Stormy Weather

DERMOT DAVIS

ISBN: 0984418113
ISBN-13: 9780984418114

DEDICATION

For Sophia.

*The Interpretation of dreams is the royal road to a
knowledge of the unconscious activities of the mind.*

~Sigmund Freud

Gail looked out the water-beaded kitchen window of
their affluent suburban home, which was just a short
commute from downtown Chicago. It just rained or maybe
it's between showers or it's possibly raining still, Gail
thought to herself. Everything was gray and wet, and it
smothered her. Her mind was becoming progressively dull,
as if everything was moving in slow motion and more and
more she was beginning not to care. About anything. It's the
medication, she decided. Increasingly she realized that she
couldn't live with it but that she couldn't live without it,
either. How on earth has it come to this, she wondered?

She looked at her husband in the window's reflection
and instantly felt weak; she just wanted to lie down and go to
bed. Oblivious to just about everything, it seemed, he sat at
the table drinking coffee with his head stuck in the
newspaper. When did he become disinterested, she asked
herself?

"Don't forget the refill on my prescription, honey," she
said, without turning around. Robert either grunted, or said,
"Oh, sure," or some such. Gail didn't listen. Another friggin'
bottle of pills. Was her depression getting any better? No. If
anything, it's getting worse, she thought. Robert isn't
concerned, she considered, because pills are his stock in
trade. From his point of view, it's perfectly natural that
people are on all kinds of pills for all kinds of mood
maladies. He's a shrink, after all. Not feeling up to par? Pop
a pill.

"I need to get to work. Where's Jason?" Robert asked,
as he finished his coffee. Gail didn't turn or respond. She
continued to wash the dishes.

Robert found the ten year old for himself. He was in the front room playing 'clap your hands,' with his imaginary friends.

"Who are you talking to?" Robert inquired.

"Just some Munchkins."

"Some Munchkins? Like in *The Wizard of Oz*?"

"They're my friends."

"They're your imaginary friends," said Robert, successfully hiding his disapproval.

"My best friends," said Jason with a broad smile. Deciding that his son obviously needed a life lesson, some instruction from his responsible parent, Robert thought quickly about what his best approach should be.

"Show them to me. What are their names?"

"Johnny, Jasper, Freddie and Ringo." Jason pointed, as he made the introductions.

"And where do these guys live?"

"Under there. Did you know that there's a huge Munchkin city right underneath the floorboards?"

"Robert failed to hide his shock upon seeing that one of the floorboards had been displaced. "You pulled up a floorboard?"

"The Munchkins did it," said Jason defensively. He could now see that his father didn't at all approve of his new friends. Robert, on the other hand, was deciding that the situation was far more serious than he had at first thought. The kid was ten years old and still believed in imaginary friends. Surely, he should have grown out of such notions at this stage. He struggled but failed to remember the stages defined in the various theories of childhood development. Pulling up floorboards took the whole imaginary friends thing to a different level. What if Jason's imaginary friends instructed him to hurt someone? Maybe even, to stab his parents to death, while they were sleeping in bed, some night?

This will not do, at all, he concluded. It's time to rid the kid of all these dangerous notions of imaginary friends, imaginary voices, imaginary everything. Besides, he'll be a teenager before too long. If he carries on with such dangerous illusions, he'll be the laughing stock of his peers. The kid has to grow up. It may seem harsh but I will actually be doing the kid a favor. As Robert got down on his knees, Gail stood watching from the doorway, unseen by her husband and child.

"Why don't you show me where all these Munchkins live," Robert said nicely, as he peered underneath the displaced floorboard.

"Right down there, in Munchkin city."

"I want you to tell me what you see, 'cause all I see are dirt and electrical wires."

Although his father's voice sounded calm, reasonable and reassuring, Jason saw the steeliness in his father's eyes and the seriousness in his expression. He now knew, he could sense, that his father was not on board with any of this. In fact, he seemed downright hostile and maybe even scary.

"Do you see a city under there?" Robert continued. "Take a good look and tell me what you see." Jason took another look. He wasn't sure why but tears formed in his eyes. Please don't let me start crying, please don't let me cry, he begged himself as, sure enough, his father said, that there was nothing, no city or anything else, underneath the floorboards; just dirt and electrical wires.

"Tell me what you see," Robert repeated.

"Nothing," Jason managed to gasp out. "Dirt and electrical wires."

Much to Jason's horror, tears streamed freely down his face. Despite his embarrassment, the good news was that they seemed to have a softening effect on his father.

"Hey, buddy, you're not in trouble. I'm doing you a favor, here. You're old enough now to distinguish between what's real and what's fantasy. Seeing little people and elves and hearing voices and stuff…" Robert didn't say childish, stupid, crazy or wrong but his tone of voice and facial expression made it entirely clear. Only whack-jobs saw stupid crap that wasn't there. Robert felt like a shit, making his kid cry like that, but he felt like he really had no choice. Sometimes making the right choice in parenting was a really tough call. Tough love. Instruction on the straight and narrow. It made for a better man.

"Come here," he said as he pulled his son into arms. "Growing up is tough and sometimes the truth really does hurt… but it's for your own good, little man."

Jason looked at his mom, who had been watching quietly from the doorway. Even though their eyes met for a few seconds, Jason was unable to read his mother. He could not tell from her glassy stare whether she was happy or sad or upset or compliant with his father's latest life lesson. Not knowing which was more terrifying: his father's take on reality or his mother's increasing distance from reality, Jason disengaged from his father's hug.

"I gotta get ready for camp."

"Sure thing, bud. I love you." He watched his son run upstairs, then noticed Gail standing in the doorway. "Everything okay?" he asked.

Gail was trying to figure out exactly what she was feeling and experiencing based upon the father-son interaction she had just witnessed. She then had what felt like an amazing realization. She almost smiled as the words left her lips; not a smile of satisfaction, per se, but rather a smile of an epiphany. It lit her up, the comprehension explained exactly what she had been trying to express for some time.

"Robert. You're turning into your father."

She wasn't trying to hurt her husband, or to be purposefully mean. She merely shared her revelation. Then, having hit the nail on the head, Gail turned and climbed the stairs.

Robert stood motionless. It was if he had just been punched hard, in the stomach. Immediately, a series of memories, made up of images, sounds, thoughts, emotions, and physical experience, flooded his mind. All of the recollections were about his father and all of them were not good. In no particular order and some heavily distorted, and fragmented, he could see his father as he saw him when he was a boy; his father's bulging eyes, as he lectured to him, his father's enormous hand, as it swung to strike him, his father's crazed twisted mouth as he yelled at him.

Robert felt weak and sick to his stomach. Was he truly turning into his father? Was he his father? As a trained psychologist, he would consider it. However, his entire being was shouting, "No, that could not be true, that could never be true!" As memories of his childhood slipped from his mind and his left brain logic slowly kicked in, he reasoned that Gail had run out of her medication and obviously was experiencing an exaggerated reality. I won't blame Gail for trying to hurt me, she's unwell, he thought. Realizing that he was now late for his first appointment, he rushed out of the house.

As Gail brushed her teeth in the bathroom upstairs, she took notice of the dark circles beneath her eyes. They seemed to be getting much darker and larger, at an alarming rate. Finished with her teeth, she reached into the medicine cabinet hoping that at least one of the many prescription pill bottles inside of it would have something in it. Discovering that they were all, as she secretly knew, empty, she rested her head against the mirror. "I can't go on like this," she reflected.

"Mom, I'm going to be late for camp, again," Jason said softly. He waited outside the closed bathroom door, coat on and backpack at the ready. "If I'm late one more time, I'll have to do clean up duty, Mr. Parker said." Concerned over the lack of response from his mom, Jason continued. "I'm covering for you, mom. You're the one that's late, not me.

9

But they don't care about that. I'll be the one who gets in trouble." Still there was no response. Jason put his ear to the door, what was she doing in there? A tiny fear of the unknown and concern for his mother crept up into his awareness.

"Are you okay, mom? I really don't care if I'm late for camp, honest. You can take your time," he said, a bit of desperation in his young voice. Then the bathroom door opened and his mom appeared. Smiling.

"You're not going to camp today," she said.

"I'm not?" Jason replied, concerned now with the turn of events. What was happening?

"Go pack your going away things. We're going to visit Aunt Margaret."

Jason sighed in relief. They were going to have an adventure. Jason beamed a bright smile and as for Gail, as soon as her last word was spoken, it was as if someone opened up a window and let some air and warm golden sunshine in.

All that we see or seem, is but a dream within a dream.

~Edgar Allan Poe

Robert drove his luxury BMW with expert speed. Coming to a four-way stop, he waited for the car on the right to cross the intersection. He could see that the female driver was nervous, uncertain about pulling out. What was she waiting for, an invite? he thought to himself. "Come on, lady," he said out loud, "rules of the road: first to stop, first to go." Giving up on her, Robert pulled out but had to brake hard when a car on his right ran through the intersection, without stopping. "Son of a bitch, that was close!" he said out loud. He gulped in air, and his heart pounded, shocked by the very close call. Turning towards the still stationery female driver, Robert yelled, "it's bad drivers like you that cause accidents!"

Not knowing exactly what he had just said, the female driver nonetheless could tell he was yelling at her. So she flipped him off. "Charming, in addition to being a competent driver, you're such a nice lady," he said out loud. Driving on, Robert checked in his glove box for some aspirin. Seeing that the bottle was empty, he chucked it into the back seat.

Although still in her twenties, Alison was an old soul. As well as being Robert's receptionist, she was the front desk reception for all three doctors which shared this floor. She was on the phone when Robert left the elevator and entered the reception area. Late, looking frazzled, Robert approached the sole patient, a female, who sat in the waiting area reading a magazine.

"So sorry to keep you waiting," Robert apologized.

"That's all right," answered the woman.

Robert belatedly realized that he did not know the woman.

"I don't know you, do I?" Robert said.

"No, I…"

"Well, I'm afraid I can't see you this morning," Robert continued. Then he spoke louder, for Alison's benefit, "I never see new patients on Mondays. I only see new patients on Wednesdays and Thursdays." Alison hung up the phone.

"Dr. Monro, Mrs. Ferguson is not…"

"I'm sorry, Mrs. Ferguson," he said smoothly, "but you'll have to reschedule for a Wednesday or a Thursday."

"But I've come all the way from Maplewood," Mrs. Ferguson protested.

"Dr. Monro, Mrs. Ferguson is not– " Alison again tried to interject, but was again cut off.

"You'll have to sharpen up, young lady," Robert said with irritation to Alison as he walked toward his office door.

"I made this appointment two weeks ago," said Mrs. Ferguson as she approached Alison's desk.

Another office door opened and Dr. Harding came and stood in his doorway. It was Dr. Harding that leased the entire floor and from whom the other doctor's had sublet from. If he didn't like a tenant, he was known not to renew their lease. From the quick glance that he gave to Robert, and the way that Robert nodded in return, it was obvious that they didn't like each other.

"Meredith Ferguson?" he announced.

"Yes?" replied Mrs. Ferguson

Dr. Harding opened his door wider, to invite her in. As she entered his office, Alison returned to opening the mail.

"I did try to tell you that she was not your patient," she said to a very embarrassed Robert.

"She must think that I'm a complete jackass," Robert said.

"I wouldn't worry about it," Alison said kindly, "Your first patient is waiting for you in your office."

"Who? Where?" asked Robert, flustered.

"Miss Blessing. In your office."

"You let Miss Blessing into my office?"

"She doesn't like the energy out here."

"She doesn't like the energy?" Robert repeated, incredulously, "so you let Miss Blessing go snooping around my office?"

"She's a very sweet lady. Be nice to her."

"She's a loony toon," said Robert, surrendering to his bad day. "You don't have any aspirin, do you?" he asked in a more conciliatory tone.

"No, sorry," replied Alison before she answered an incoming call.

Robert quietly and slowly turned the handle on his office door and then quickly opened it as if to catch his patient doing something she wasn't supposed be doing. An elegant lady, in her fifties, Miss Blessing stood holding a framed photograph of Robert and his family.

"This must have been taken back in happier times," she said, "before you started turning into your father."

Robert was closing the door as she spoke and wasn't quite sure that he heard her correctly. "What did you say? What did you just say?" he asked, aghast.

"I said that this picture must have been taken back in happier times." Then she looked at him, curiously.

Robert took the framed snapshot from her hands and glanced at it. It was an early photo of him and Gail with their newborn Jason.

"You're smiling in the picture," Miss Blessing said. Sure enough he was and he did indeed look a great deal happier when he was younger. Based upon her photographed demeanor, so did Gail.

"Why don't you take a seat?" Robert said and directed her to the chair opposite. Then he placed the framed photo back on the shelf. On the same shelf sat Robert's published, academic books: *Freud's Interpretation of Dreams, a Critique*; *Dreams and the Psychoanalytical Method*; *Dream Symbolism and Hysteria*, and off to the side, as if in its own, perhaps lesser, category, *The Complete Moron's Guide to Dream Interpretation*.

"I'd like to continue where I left off the last time, if that's alright with you," said Miss Blessing, settling in carefully.

"Fine with me, as long as you know that without medication, your situation is… untenable."

"Untenable is not a word in my vocabulary, doctor," the patient responded.

"You don't agree?"

"Oh, I'm not disagreeing. The word is not in my vocabulary because I don't know what it means."

"What I'm trying to say is that I have nothing more to offer you unless you agree to medication. Analysis can only go so far. Only drugs can effect a re-balancing of brain chemistry."

"They've just released my book, by the way," interjected Miss Blessing, leaping completely off topic, "my sessions with you have provided me with such fabulous ideas."

"That's great," said Robert, his face and tone of voice showing no enthusiasm.

"There's something wrong with my brain chemistry?"

"Let me put it this way. My son sees imaginary friends."

"That's wonderful," she said and smiled.

"For a ten year old, seeing things that don't exist is relatively normal. For a fifty-plus year old woman, it's a chemical imbalance in the brain."

"Wasn't it Shakespeare who said that there are more things in heaven and earth than are dreamt of in your philosophy?"

"Indeed it was, I use that same quote in one of my books."

"Well, then," said Miss Blessing, resting her case.

"In my book, I describe Hamlet as a classic manic-depressive," he added, as if implying that Hamlet would have been a prime candidate for modern medication. "Look, as we've discussed, your problem is that you can't delineate dreams from reality. To you, by your own admission, everything is a dream."

"A dream within a dream," said Miss Blessing, clarifying.

"Which, technically, based upon your understanding and experience of reality means that you are delusional or suffering from delusional tendencies."

"I see."

For further explanation, Robert formed two fists. "This fist represents the dream world and this other fist represents the real world," he said and lifted each fist alternately to punctuate his words. "Standing in the real world, I look into the dream world. I can identify certain images and symbols

14

that have meaning to me in the real world. Dream interpretation only works if I can compare one to the other. Do you understand?"

Miss Blessing seemed to be having a hard time with his analogy. Robert went further and joined his two fists together.

"If both of them, the reality and the dream, get mixed up... well, then, heaven help us. We can't tell real from symbol, the actual thing from its shadow."

Despite Robert's obvious frustration with her inability to accept his words, and ignoring his annoyance, she was enjoying the conversation. Meanwhile, Robert rummaged about in his desk drawer for some aspirin.

"What if we woke up from this dream that we call reality only to find ourselves in another dream?" Miss Blessing smiled, proud of her thought progression, "we're living in a dream, within a dream. Have you lost something, doctor?"

"Aspirin. I have a splitting headache." Miss Blessing took out a pouch from her purse. "You have aspirin?" Robert asked, hopefully.

"Essence of rose quartz," replied Miss Blessing, "as harmless as homeopathy."

"I don't believe in homeopathy," said Robert dismissively, then, more desperately, "but will they cure a headache?"

Miss Blessing poured the powder into a glass of water. They fizzed and sparkled.

"What are they?"

"Perfectly safe, Robert. I take them every day."

Robert took up the glass and inspected it. The water was now clear. He smelled it.

"Seems harmless enough. If this saves me a visit to the pharmacy, I owe you," Robert said. Then he downed the entire glass in one gulp. He waited a moment, his head tilted slightly to one side. Alas, he felt no different.

"It's tasteless. I don't feel anything."

"Give it time, Robert."

Robert put away the glass and, getting back to business, looked at his notes.

"Where were we?"

"We were talking about waking up from our pain, opening up our hearts to a greater understanding of reality."

"We were?" asked Robert, now feeling somewhat groggy. He squinted his eyes as if trying to focus on something, behind Miss Blessing, at the rear of the room.

"What is it? Do you see something?"

Robert rubbed his eyes, as if to orient himself. He felt sure that he saw a white, ethereal, cloud-like figure move in through a door and exit through another.

"I should mention that you may start seeing things you've never seen before," said Miss Blessing, preparing to leave, "don't get up, I can see my own way out." He glanced at the clock. Curiously, their time together was up.

As Miss Blessing left the office, Robert remained seated. He felt very woozy.

Between the dreams of night and day there is not so great a difference.

~Carl Jung

Gail and Jason were met at the Los Angeles airport by Gail's older sister, Margaret. Although Margaret was bossy, opinionated and never shy about telling Gail how best to live her life, Gail still felt that the change of scene would do her and Jason a world of good. Back at Margaret's house, Gail prepared herself for the questions and the inevitable advice. As Jason amused himself in the front room with a video game, upstairs, Margaret helped her sister unpack.

"Why don't you leave him, for good? He obviously doesn't make you happy, anymore."

"I'm not ruling it out, Meg. I'm not ruling anything out, at this stage."

"Probably the only thing helping you tolerate your bad marriage are those anti-depressants he's had you doped up on. For crying out loud, what kind of a long term situation is that? If you find yourself trapped, find a way out."

"I'm not so sure that I can blame it all on Robert, Meg. I have my own issues to take a look at," Gail admitted.

"Such as?" her sister said, as if she was entirely prepared to put all of the blame on her sister's husband.

"I just need some time to think, a change of scene from the same old, same old," replied Gail tactfully. She wasn't prepared to go into detail with her sister, at least not at this stage.

"Don't talk to me about same old, same old," stated Margaret, "my life is just one big, same old." She laughed to herself. Then, as if a light bulb had gone off in her mind, Margaret suddenly became excited. "Oh my god, it's perfect!" she said, beaming.

"What is?"

"I was checking out last minute cruises on the web and right then, you called me. What would you say to a five day cruise? On me!" Clearly excited, she looked as if she meant it.

This was the wildest and most unexpected thing Gail had been offered since a student in college. The ultimate escape, a reprieve from life, at no financial cost to herself. She knew it was impossible but part of her was intrigued.

"I couldn't go away on a cruise just now, Meg. What about Jason? And Bob... my responsibilities... your responsibilities? Don't you have to work?"

"I haven't had work in months," replied Margaret.

She ran from the room. Gail followed. Excited, Margaret grabbed her laptop, and began checking travel websites, "interior design is in a bit of a slump, these days."

Margaret's cell phone rang. She pulled it out and a glance revealed that it was Robert calling. She didn't say anything to Gail, except to make a privacy gesture and quickly left the room.

"Hello?" she answered brightly.

Robert stood in his empty home, a hand written note in his hand. He was perplexed, sad, angry, lonely and just plain confused, all rolled into one. Where was his family?

"Margaret, it's Robert," he said, knowing quite well that his number had come up on her cell phone, "Gail's phone is turned off and I have a note here saying that she's gone to visit you?"

"Yes, Robert, she's here, safe and sound but she's sleeping and I don't want to wake the poor girl, she seems especially exhausted," Margaret lied. Gail could hear her sister and realizing that it was her husband on the line, she joined her in the hall and stretched out her hand to take the phone. Margaret, however, waved her off.

"Will I tell her that you called?" Margaret said chirpily.

Exasperated beyond words, Robert restrained himself by not calling her a lying, interfering bitch, which was right there on the tip of his tongue.

"Yes. Tell her that I called. And that I love her. And Jason too, of course," Robert blubbered, almost hating his weakness. He hung up right away, without giving her a chance to say anything else in that fake, cheerful voice of hers. He certainly didn't want her to hear the quivering in his voice and sense that he had tears in his eyes. Hanging up, he wiped them away.

Gail gave Margaret a stern look as her sister hung up the phone and retreated back to the bedroom. "You could have let me speak to him," she said with little enthusiasm, "he's probably very worried."

"He just wanted to be certain that you made it okay and that you were safe. I assured him on all fronts. There's lots of time to talk to your hubby, sweetie. You just got here…

oh, my god, you won't believe this deal," she exclaimed as something on the web caught her eye, "we're going to Mexico!" Jason walked into the room just in time to hear the word, "Mexico."

Before Gail could decide for herself or object to any portion of it, with a click of several keys Margaret had booked them on a cruise. Then with the self-satisfaction of a cat, she smiled hugely at her sister.

"Am I going too?" Jason inquired, nervously.

"Yes, sweetie, of course you're going too. We're all going… to Mexico!" She pronounced Mexico with an "h" and, suddenly feeling energized, jumped up.

Margaret took Jason's hands in hers and together they danced a happy dance all the while shouting, "Mexico! Mexico!" with an "h" instead of an "x." Gail sat watching them both. Going on a cruise would have been unthinkable yesterday, or even several hours ago, she thought. But the happiness of her sister and her son was infectious and truthfully, maybe fun, sunshine, and spending time with people who really and truly loved her was just what the doctor ordered. So, finally, after many weeks, perhaps even months, Gail allowed herself a broad, satisfying smile and relaxed into the moment.

> *Much of our waking experience is but a dream in the daylight.*
>
> ~George Eliot

Robert sat across from his youngest patient, Edward. At ten years of age, the boy already had the attitude and emotions of a rebellious teenager. Robert listened attentively as Edward related his latest dream.

"Then I turn the corner but they're still following me," he said, the frightening nature of the sinister dream still very present for him.

"How do you know that 'they're still following' you? Can you see them?"

"I don't have to turn around to see them," Edward said angrily, losing patience with Robert's line of questioning. "I know that that they're still there. Two of them."

"How do you know that there's two of them?"

"I just know, okay?"

"Okay," said Robert in a soothing voice, "then what happens?"

"Just as I turn the corner, all of a sudden, I'm in a huge forest."

"What's happening in the forest?" asks Robert.

"What's happening in the forest?" repeats Edward, as if that is the most inane question he has ever heard, "I'm being chased. I'm still being chased, except now I'm in a forest."

"I see," said Robert, not wanting to lose his patient, "are you still being chased by the same people or things?"

"I can hear their breathing. It's horrible. They sound like dragons."

"What does a dragon sound like?"

Edward looked at Robert like he was a total moron.

"I don't know," he answered, "like dragons."

"Okay, no problem. Continue. You're scared…"

"Of course I'm scared," said Edward, his patience almost entirely gone, "I'm running through a dark forest being chased by two fire-breathing dragons, what do you think I'm feeling?"

Robert ignored Edward's reaction and attitude and kept his voice and demeanor even-keel.

"And just as they're about to catch you, you wake up…" he adds, helpfully.

"I fall first. And then when I'm about to look up…I wake up."

Edward's voice broke then and his show of bravado, the thin veneer of daring he'd worn while sharing his dream, was shattered by the tears of the frightened little boy that he actually was. Robert passed him a box of tissues. Edward took one and blew his nose loudly.

Robert then, to his great shock, was certain that he saw something move right behind Edward. He focused his eyes and squinted. He saw an ethereal shape, almost cloud-like, but he decided that it looked like a woman in flowing veils. As Edward threw the soiled tissue onto his desk, the shape disappeared.

"How often do you have this dream, or something similar?" Robert asked, regaining his composure.

"I don't know. All the time, I guess."

"It's a very common dream, you know. Being chased by monsters you can't see. Lots of people have dreams like this, people of all ages."

"Do you have them?"

"Sure. Sometimes. Not in a while, but I used to."

"Did you get scared?"

"Oh, sure. You wouldn't be human, if you didn't get scared."

"Did you wet the bed?"

"Not lately," he paused and then gently asked, "Do you?"

Edward was too embarrassed to reply. Robert took that as a yes.

"Let me tell you what I do, Edward. This is going to sound difficult, and it is, but it's very effective. You don't want to have these dreams, anymore, do you?"

"I think that's why my mom brought me here, Dr. Monro," Edward said cheekily.

"Dreams are important because they give us valuable information about our lives. When they're scary dreams... sometimes it means that there's something in our lives that frightens us but that we're ignoring or denying because they are too fearful for us to face up to or maybe we aren't aware that we're afraid." Robert knew that he was not explaining himself very well at all. Edward's perplexed expression confirmed this.

"So, there's something in my life that I'm not facing up to?" asked Edward, struggling to understand the therapist.

"Exactly," said Robert.

"What?"

"What are you not facing up to?" Robert clarified, "that, I do not know."

"But you just said that lots of people have the exact same dream!" Deflated, Edward sank deeper into his chair. He was trying very hard but this was very distressing for him.

"Lots of people have similar dreams but the information, the message for each of them, is not the same. The dragons may be the same but what they represent is different for everybody."

"I don't know what you're talking about, this is stupid," Edward said wearily.

"Let's say, if I had that dream, I'm being chased by dragons... maybe I'm worried about paying the mortgage or my bills. See, then the dragons maybe represent the landlord or the bank, you see? For you, maybe you're afraid of being picked on by those two bullies, what are their names?"

"Brent and Randy."

"Brent and Randy," repeated Robert, hoping he successfully got his message across.

"You think the dragons are really Brent and Randy?"

"Could be. The only way to know for sure is to ask them."

"You want me to ask Brent and Randy if they're really dragons?" Edward asked incredulously.

"No," explained Robert, talking more slowly, and trying to choose his words more carefully, "I want you to ask the dragons who they are... in your dream."

"How do I do that?"

"This is the difficult part. You have to stop running in the dream and instead, turn around and face them."

Robert paused, allowing Edward to digest this new information. He didn't want to lose the boy now, now that he might finally be able to give him some valuable tools that would help him cope.

"Turn around and face them?" Edward repeated, hoping it would begin to make more sense to him.

"Exactly. You don't even know if they really are dragons, do you?"

"But I'm asleep, Dr. Monro. How can I ask…"

"By waking up in your dream," said Robert, putting a final postscript on the concept.

"Waking up in the dream?" said Edward, now completely lost.

"Before you go to sleep, tell yourself that you're going to turn around and, when you get the chance, ask these dragons what it is that they really want. Keep saying to yourself, 'Stop running. Turn around. Take charge.' Then, when you wake up during your dream, even though you are still asleep, you'll remember what to do."

Robert leaned back, happy with his explanation. "I bet that you'll find that they're not dragons, at all."

"But what if I stop running and I turn around and then they eat me, or something?" Edward inquired with all seriousness.

"Let me tell you something important," Robert continued, "you cannot be eaten in your sleep. Nobody has ever died in a dream. It's not possible."

"How do you know?" asked Edward, wanting greater reassurance than hearsay.

"Because you always wake up just before you think you're going to die. The worst thing that can happen to you in a dream is that you wake up. Isn't that something?" Robert concluded, somewhat smugly.

"I guess," responded Edward, uncertain.

"Dreams are puzzles of the mind, Edward. Puzzles, nothing more. Ever done a crossword puzzle?"

"No. But I know what it is."

"Any puzzle, a jigsaw puzzle, a riddle…" said Robert, running out of analogies, "you're given a set of clues, you think about it, you work it out. No one ever died from doing a jigsaw puzzle, did they?"

"I don't know," answered Edward, still unsure about the entire thing. None of it was making much sense to him.

"I know that it all seems scary but you're a brave young man and I know that you're going to do just fine. In fact, I have something for you." Robert reached into his drawer and took out an attractive, colorful picture of St. George slaying the dragon. Edward leaned forward and grinned. It was obvious that he immediately liked it.

"That's Saint George. He became famous for slaying dragons. Ever hear of him?"

Edward was too engrossed in checking out the beautiful detail of the picture to answer.

"Hang it over your bed. It will give you courage. Now, see you next week?"

"Edward carefully handled the illustration, not wanting to smudge it, as he made his way to the office door. Robert stood and followed the patient.

"Remember, Edward. Stop running. Turn around. Take charge!"

Edward nodded and left. Happy with himself, Robert closed the door behind Edward. His cell phone rang and, after checking and recognizing the caller ID, he took the call straight away.

"Hello, mum," he answered cheerfully. His mood changed instantly to one of concern, however, as he listened to his mother.

"I'll be right there," he said curtly and with a worried expression on his face, hung up.

Dreaming or awake, we perceive only events that have meaning to us.

~Jane Roberts

Robert had Alison cancel two appointments. Then he rushed to the hospital. Walking briskly down the hospital corridor, he found his aging mother, Anita, sitting on a bench. She looked bereft and gray with concern.

"Mother," he said, and awkwardly hugged her.

"He's in there all alone, but they won't let me in there so that I can be with him," she said, obviously very distraught. Her nose was pink and her eyes a bit swollen, as if she had been crying. Through the glass, Robert could see his father, attached to all kinds of machines, sleeping.

"They probably need him to get some rest. What happened?"

"It's a stroke, I think," she said unsurely, as if no one had updated her about her husband's condition. "Somebody should be in there with him."

"He's sleeping, mother. It's for the best," Robert said, more to reassure than to take the side of the doctors. "I'm certain that his physicians know what they're doing."

Seeing no other way to alleviate his mother's suffering or worries, he looked up and down the corridor quickly, then, when he saw no one who was obviously a hospital employee, opened the door and ushered his mother inside the hospital room.

"They said we shouldn't…"

"Never mind what they said," Robert interjected, "I'm a doctor."

Anita was about to argue and remind him that he was a doctor of the mind and not of the body but quickly decided against it. This was her opportunity to be close to her husband again. Her son could do the talking, when the nurses come to angrily shoo us out, she decided. Looking at her husband, asleep and helpless, filled her with dread. What if he never wakes up? What if he wakes up and he's an invalid or brain damaged and maybe doesn't even remember me? What will I do then? I'll be all alone, same as if he passed, except he'll be in a body needing constant care and attention. She could barely face the thought of any of it.

"What if he doesn't…?" she said to Robert but was unable to finish the sentence.

"What did the doctor say, exactly?" Robert asked as he looked over the chart at the base of the bed. His training, however, was not adequate enough for him to decipher much of it.

"She did say that there's something wrong with his kidneys," she said, trying to remember, although due to shock over his collapse, and her fatigue, her mind had been in no state to hear and understand medical information at the time. "They're not working the way they should… his kidneys."

Robert knew that he really needed to hear what was wrong straight from the doctor, herself.

"Why don't you stay with dad and I'll go and find her?" he said to his mother, looking on the chart to see if he could find the doctor's last name. The thought of being left alone in the room, the room that she was told she should not be in, filled her with much anxiety.

"We shouldn't be in here," she said, a nervous tremor in her voice.

Robert was so focused upon his task that he didn't pick up on her nervousness or maybe he didn't think it relevant. Either way, he decided that he must find the doctor and learn exactly what was going on with his father. How serious is this? he wondered as he left his mother and father behind and exited the room. Once outside the hospital room, he looked around to orient himself. Looking down the end of the corridor, he saw that same ethereal shape, what he was now calling in his mind, 'The Elusive Lady,' as she exited to the stairwell. Without consciously deciding to do so, he quickly followed her.

Once in the stairwell, he discovered it empty. Looking down the stairwell, as if gazing into a gloomy deep well, Robert saw the door to the basement closing. He ran down the stairs and went through the door. The door led to a long corridor in the cold, dank basement. Where did she go? He saw a door closing to his right. As he approached it he noticed that the sign on the wall read, 'Morgue.' He slowly entered. No one was around which made the place seem even more creepy and ghostlike.

Curiously, there was no sign of his Elusive Lady. Several dead bodies lay covered on gurneys. In his mind, he believed that he was led here for a purpose, except he didn't know just what that could be. Perhaps I would know one of the deceased, he reflected. He lifted one of the sheets covering a nearby corpse but, not knowing the person, immediately freaked. In disgust, he dropped the cloth and quickly left.

Dreaming men are haunted men.

~Stephen Vincent Benét

The first thing that Robert did when he got back to his home was call Gail. Yet again, he got the same impersonal voice mail recording. Obviously, her phone was still switched off. His professional self reassured him that it wasn't that she didn't love him anymore but rather that she just needed some space. Everybody needs space at some time or another, he reasoned. The absence of Gail and Jason made Robert feel uneasy in his own house. The place felt empty and too quiet and somehow darker than normal inside. It just did not feel right without them there. In the front room, he noticed that the same floorboard had again been removed.

Didn't I replace that this morning? he asked himself. He looked around at the hardwood floors, as if for the first time. These were the original wooden floorboards and some of them were not in the best condition. He remembered that having them completely replaced, an expensive, time-consuming and disruptive endeavor, was on his household 'to do' list.

I guess I never got around to it, he realized. He couldn't remember the last time that he spent some significant time in the front room. He carefully put back the floorboard back into place and wondered to himself what he was going to eat for supper.

That night, Robert slept uneasily. As he slept, four tiny people — Munchkins — appeared in his room and began to goof around. One of them swung on the bed headboard. To the amusement of the others, another Munchkin mimicked the way Robert was sleeping, making similar facial expressions, and generally mocked him. A moment later, the Munchkin on the headboard fell off and landed upon Robert's pillow, with a little thump, very narrowly missing Robert's head. When it appeared as if he were about to wake, the other Munchkins stopped —motionless. Just before Robert opened his eyes, they all scampered under the bed and missed detection by a split second.

Sensing that something was awry, Robert looked around the room. Seeing that nothing was amiss, he quickly shut his eyes again. The Munchkins slowly and quietly inched out from beneath the bed and left the room.

The next morning, in the middle of preparing his morning breakfast – bagel and coffee – Robert walked out of the front door of the house to grab the newspaper. As he returned, heading back toward the kitchen, he glanced into the front room. He suddenly stopped in his tracks: the same floorboard was again displaced. This time, however, there was no doubt in his mind.

He definitely remembered that he had carefully replaced the floorboard the previous evening. How then, could this be explained? Walking closer, he scanned the area for clues. It had to be done by a human hand, but whose? Was it possible that someone had broken into the house in the night? He glanced at the front windows, and all around. Everything seemed locked and secure, just the way it had been when he went to bed last night. Jason was with his mom, so that rules him out. Was someone else playing a practical joke? And if so, who? Could someone still be in his house?

Robert searched every room in his home and made certain to check every window in every room. Nothing looked suspicious or out of place. This is just plain weird, he decided. He put the floorboard back into its place and went back into the kitchen and packed his bagel and coffee to go.

A disconcerting sense of unease, which he was unable to shake, stayed with Robert. He felt emotionally off, even as his first client, fifty-five year old Tony Applegate, sat across from him and described his latest dream with much enthusiasm.

"And then, I find myself in bed with my wife's sister," Tony said, expecting a bigger reaction from Robert than the seeming disinterest that he seemed to be getting. "What do you think it means?"

"You're having an affair with your wife's sister?" asked Robert. Distracted, he was half in and half out of the conversation.

"In the dream," emphasized Tony, "but not in real life, no, absolutely not."

"Yes, you're having an affair with your sister-in-law in the dream," clarified Robert, trying to stay present, "go on."

"Well, that's it," replied Tony, hoping for greater feedback.

"What are you feeling, in the dream?"

"That's just it, in the dream I'm loving every minute of it. I'm not feeling one bit guilty. Weird, huh?"

"Are you thinking of having an affair with your wife's sister?"

"Of course not. I'm perfectly happy with Amy. She's my soul mate. You know that."

To Robert's shock, the Elusive Lady, now more tangible than ethereal, walked straight through the door and appeared at the rear of the room. Although her face was veiled, he was immediately struck that she was the most beautiful woman that he had ever seen. Robert watched her sit in an armchair just to the left of his client Tony. Her presence seemed to affect everything in the room; it was as if a light of love, an intangible yet powerful energy of loving adoration, had entered the room and raised the vibration of everything in and around the space. Her nearness to Tony, unbeknownst to him, filled him with waves of love.

"You know what?" Tony continued, incredulously, "I love her. I love her."

"You love who?" Robert asked, trying to concentrate, keep watch on the Elusive Lady, and maintain a tenuous hold on his sanity. "You love your wife?"

"I love my wife," said Tony joyfully, "I love my wife's sister. I love them both."

Try as he might, Robert could not take his eyes off the Elusive Lady. She sat with poise, balanced on the armchair, a tender smile on her lips. Tony followed Robert's eyes to the armchair and was puzzled about his therapist's lack of focus upon his issues. Robert wondered if Tony was seeing what he was seeing.

"What do you think of that armchair?" Robert asked, fishing.

Tony was so thrown by the peculiar question that he wasn't sure he could possibly have heard the doc right.

"What was the question?" Tony asked innocently.

"That armchair over there. What images do you get when you look at it?" asked Robert, masking his interest to make it sound as if the question had some therapeutic relevance. Tony checked out the chair, and saw just an empty armchair, unaware that the Elusive Lady was looking at him with an exceedingly loving expression.

"It's beautiful," said Tony, smiling goofily, "it's the most beautiful armchair I've ever seen in my life." To his surprise, he meant it. He felt a wave of love for the piece of furniture.

"It looks... empty to you?" asked Robert, wondering if perhaps Tony might be seeing something, anything, a shape, ethereal or otherwise, occupying the chair.

"How do you mean?"

"Who do you see sitting in it? For instance."

The more Tony looked at the armchair, the more it became beautiful to him, so much so that now it appeared to him as if the seat were glowing.

"I could see myself sitting in that baby," he said, now desiring it, "I'd sit in it all day. In fact, I want to go sit in it, right now. How much do you want for it?" He was entirely serious.

"It's not for sale," Robert said dismissively, "but your answers were very helpful in analyzing your dream. Continue where you left off. You were in bed with your wife's sister?"

Now in a state of bliss, Tony felt love for everybody and everything. He looked lovingly at Robert. He felt as if he were having some kind of breakthrough. To his great surprise, this therapy thing was having a real positive effect on him.

"I just want to say that I love you, Dr. Monro. I've never said that to a grown man before but I love you." Tony couldn't help himself but he just had to get up and go over and give Dr. Monro a big man hug. "You've helped me so much..." he said, tearfully.

Robert did his best to accept Tony's upwelling of emotion but still could not stop focusing upon the Elusive

Lady. She looked at him lovingly and tenderly. What is happening to my world? he wondered to himself.

Dreams are more real than reality itself, they're closer to the self.

~Gao Xingjian

Robert couldn't face another evening alone in his home, so he invited his former mentor, Professor Heathcliff, to stop by for a quiet dinner. Since Robert didn't cook, he brought back some upscale Italian food that he ordered in advance and picked up on his way home. After a delicious meal, they retired to the front room. Robert poured two brandies.

"What's the latest on your father?" Heathcliff asked.

"Still no change," answered Robert, handing a glass to Heathcliff.

"I'm sorry to hear that," said Heathcliff, without much conviction.

"He'll come out of it. He's got so much anger inside of him, he's not going to stay quiet for too long."

"And Gail?" asked Heathcliff.

"She's…" Robert didn't really know what the deal was with Gail or where her head was at. "I don't know. She won't take my calls and her busy-body sister is probably doing a darn good assassination attempt on my character, no doubt trying to convince her to leave me."

"You're really going through it, huh?" said Heathcliff. He hoped that Robert would switch gears. He liked to stay in touch with star pupils but preferred those that graduated to peers. He did not want the evening to devolve into a glorified therapy session.

"Well, that's not all of it," said Robert, directing Heathcliff to sit. Behind Monro, the four Munchkins waltzed in.

"They're throwing you out of the building?" said Heathcliff, attempting to preempt Robert's next tale of woe. Robert reacted with shock and surprise.

"No. Who told you that?"

"Just a nasty rumor going around," said Heathcliff dismissively, not wanting to go into it, "it's probably nothing. What else?"

Robert hesitated but he didn't know any other way of putting it. "I think this house is haunted," he said, as casually as he could muster.

Taken aback, Heathcliff wasn't quite sure how to respond.

"I know, I know, I don't believe in these things, either," said Robert now regretting even mentioning it, "or someone's playing practical jokes."

"What kind of jokes?" asked Heathcliff, more easily able to accept some unknown prankster as an explanation for strange goings on.

"I find my boy, Jason, looking down underneath the floorboards. There's a floorboard pulled up. He tells me that the 'Munchkins' did it." Just as he spoke, a Munchkin ran through the room being chased by the other three. Neither human male noticed.

"The Munchkins?" asked Heathcliff.

"These imaginary friends. He calls them Munchkins."

"That's pretty common, imaginary friends," said Heathcliff, happy to be upon what now was clearly more familiar ground.

"So, I put the floorboard back and go to bed," continued Robert, "and the next morning, the floorboard is pulled up. I put back the floorboard and go to work. I come back in the evening, the floorboard is pulled back up again. I have a security system on the house, a mouse couldn't get in here without me knowing about it. There's no rational explanation."

Still unseen by the two human men, the four Munchkins ran back through the room.

"A haunted house is a rational explanation?" questioned a skeptical Heathcliff.

"More rational than a bunch of Munchkins," said Robert, turning and now seeing something — a Munchkin — run through the room. In shock, he dropped his glass.

"What's the matter?" asked Heathcliff, and turned to look in the direction that Robert was staring.

"You don't see them?"

"See who?"

The other Munchkins ran in and grabbed their tiny friend.

"Holy crap, there's four of them," said Robert.

"You've got bugs of some kind?" asked Heathcliff, trying to see what Robert was seeing.

"No, not bugs. Munchkins. Right there," said Robert, pointing.

"Munchkins?" asked Heathcliff, totally puzzled.

Angrily, Robert swept his arms wide in an effort to scare them off.

"Whoosh, whoosh. Get the hell out of here!" he yelled. The Munchkins ran off. Concerned for Robert's sanity, which he seemed to be losing, Heathcliff stood up.

"For heaven's sake, Robert. You're under way too much stress. Calm down."

Robert collected himself, realizing how things must seem like to someone that couldn't see what he could see.

"I'm sorry. I've been... I guess I am a bit stressed." He poured some new brandies for each of them.

"Why don't I prescribe something for you? Until you get things back in order again."

"No. No, thanks. I'm fine," protested Robert, "I haven't been sleeping well, that's all. I'm fine." Heathcliff didn't insist. The remainder of their time together was quite awkward, almost uncomfortable. They talked only of superficial things. When Heathcliff finally took his leave, Robert decided to have a final glass of brandy as a nightcap. Not used to drinking quite so much, feeling more drained and woozy, he sat and finally stretched out on the sofa. Unable to keep his eyes open, he fell asleep.

Sometime in the AM, Robert awoke. His eyes opened slowly, his mind struggling to orient to the unfamiliar sleeping space. Standing in the doorway, in semi darkness, the Elusive Lady glowed in all her magnificence. As he sat up, she walked away.

"No, wait!" he shouted, and struggled to get to his feet. He stepped on the displaced floorboard which flipped up and banged him in the head. "Ouch!" Stumbling backward, he stepped into the open gap, fell through it and vanished from sight.

With a splash, Robert found himself in complete darkness under water; he splashed his way through the murky liquid towards the surface. Strands of what looked like seaweed and other dark undersea vegetable matter gave the water an eerie look. Dark forms appeared to swim near the bottom of this place. They, whatever they were, further panicked Robert. Kicking his legs and pumping his arms as hard and fast as he could, he managed to surface. Taking deep, terrified breaths, he made his way to the grass verge. He looked around. He appeared to be on the edge of a pond in a desolate countryside that he did not recognize.

There were no signs of buildings or lights, just the full moon and the sound of frogs and crickets. He now heard the distant baying of a pack of coyotes or wolves, he couldn't be certain which. He touched the grass. It felt entirely too real to be a dream. But how on earth could he fall through the floorboards of his residence in suburbia and end up... here? Wherever here was. Still wet, he shivered a bit.

What was happening? It has got to be a dream, he decided because otherwise it makes no sense, whatsoever. Suddenly there was a thump! The earth beneath him shook.

He looked about and listened, on full alert. Thump! Thump! If he didn't know any better, his first guess was that a dinosaur was approaching. Was he dreaming of Jurassic Park? Thump! Thump! Thump! Thump!

Holy crap, some voice within him said, that's no dinosaur, that's a dragon! One, maybe more. As the foot thumps got louder and closer, Robert ran for his life.

Running for the shelter of trees, he entered a wooded area. They must have seen him or sniffed out his presence, he decided, as the foot thumps got faster and came closer and closer. They got so close that he could hear breathing and a terrifying bellowing sound, or whatever that god-awful noise was, that they emitted. Were they communicating or was that just their natural rapid hunting cry? he wondered. The forest was dark and the undergrowth thick. It was very hard going. So much so that Robert got entangled in the undergrowth, tripped and fell. He immediately got to his feet and ran again, not even stopping to see if he was hurt. The awful sounds of their heavy inhalations and the increased rhythm of their feet grew more and more intense.

Robert's heart beat so fast that he was sure it was going to burst out of his chest or stop altogether. Flop! He fell flat on his face again and, this time, his feet were so intertwined in gnarly green, sticky undergrowth that he was not easily able to get up. He panicked. It was too late to hide now as they were upon him. He shielded his head with his arms and found himself screaming at the top of his lungs in terror. Thump! Thump! Thump! Thump! They came closer and he thought that he would surely die.

Thump! Robert opened his eyes in pain to discover he had fallen off of the sofa in his living room. Drenched in sweat, his throat felt scratchy, and he cursed himself! Damn it, I was dreaming! He didn't know whether to feel relieved that he wasn't about to be eaten by dragons or to chastise himself for not realizing that he was dreaming when it was so obviously a dream, and a badly imagined one at that. He was the dream expert, after all.

As he made his way to the kitchen, for some badly needed coffee, he tried to remember the last time he had such an intense, terrible dream. He couldn't recall the occasion. Boy, did he miss Gail and Jason. As soon as it was a decent hour, Robert called Gail's phone again. He got her voice mail:

"Hi, thanks for calling. Meg, Gail and Jason have gone on a cruise, lucky us. Leave a message if it's important and I'll get back to you as soon as I can."

"A cruise?" Robert said aloud, "seriously?" Then he hung up, without leaving a message.

All men whilst they are awake are in one common world: but each of them, when he is asleep, is in a world of his own.

~Plutarch

Gail, Meg and Jason lay on loungers on the sun deck, or rather, one of the many beautiful sun decks on the huge ship. A waiter, in a crisp clean uniform, delivered their drink orders. Jason noticed some fruit and a colorful little paper umbrella on a wooden toothpick-like stick stuck in his tall glass and figured that he was getting someone else's drink.

"Mine was a coke, sir," he said, playing a grown up in his head.

"That is a coke, sir," the waiter said kindly.

"Oh," said Jason, "thank you." This cruise is really cool, he thought.

When Jason excused himself to go to the bathroom, it gave Meg a chance to check in with her younger sister. "Are you liking this?" she asked, fishing for a compliment.

"What's not to like?" replied Gail, taking a sip from her drink.

"You don't hate it, then. That's good, I suppose," Meg said.

"Thank you so much for splashing out on this trip. It's doing Jason and I a world of good and I don't regret it for a second," said Gail, realizing that that was what Meg really wanted to hear. Sure enough, her sister smiled broadly, then breathed in the fresh sea air.

"I just love cruises," she said, "thank you both for keeping me company. I wouldn't have done this by myself." She lay back on her lounger and tilted her large-brimmed sun hat down over her eyes just a bit. The day was crisp, clear and sunny.

"Anything to help you out," said Gail, with a conspiratorial grin. She looked down at her lightly tanned legs. It would be time to turn over soon.

"You look a million times better," Meg said, taking a hard look at her sister, "the sea air and liberal doses of sunshine obviously agree with you."

"Robert must think I've lost it," Gail said, feeling some guilt, "vanishing like that was pretty mean. Leaving him a note and nothing else? It was pretty cruel, when I think about it. I could have made a simple phone call."

"Every marriage needs a good shake up, now and again. He won't take you for granted so easily in the future."

Gail knew that Robert was not solely to blame for their marital issues but she really didn't want to get into it with her sister, who had never married. In fact, Meg's relationship history was spotty, at best. She didn't seem to understand give and take or personal responsibility. Traditionally, Gail never had taken any of the relationship advice Meg had to offer with any degree of seriousness.

Despite the guilt she felt about leaving Robert, without so much as a phone call, she also intuitively knew that what she was doing was beneficial to them both. It was very healing for her personally and would ultimately help with their marital problems. She was ready to give things another go, even if it meant another round of couples counseling upon her return. All she knew was that she left on an impulse she felt that she had to follow.

For now, she was going to think and talk about anything else other than her marriage with Robert. Besides, she considered, lying in the sun on the deck of a cruise ship drinking Bloody Marys in the afternoon was not at all conducive to a heart-to-heart chat about marital problems, or indeed any problems at all, for that matter.

Jason came back from the bathroom and settled down to read. He looked so healthy with his smiling sun-browned face. They had swum in one of several swimming pools every day, and eaten lots of fresh fruits and veggies. They had gone to shows and even stayed up late to go to a midnight chocolate buffet. In the mornings she and Meg had walked around the ship on the running/jogging track. She felt energized and fitter than she had in a long time. She was amazed at what a rejuvenating, energizing, relaxing and other wise perfect time-out this cruise was turning out to be and did not, for one second, regret leaving her husband behind.

We are such stuff, As dreams are made on; and our little life, Is rounded with a sleep.

~William Shakespeare

Late for work again, Robert quickly reversed out of his driveway in the beemer, causing an oncoming car to swerve in order to avoid crashing into him. The driver honked, belatedly, more as a show of disapproval than as a safety precaution. Robert took a deep breath and thanked the universe in general for his near miss.

Coming to the dreaded four-way stop near his home, Robert brought his vehicle to a halt. He waited for the car to his right. The vehicle had arrived first or at about the same time that he had. He waited for it to pull out but it didn't move. For some reason, it really annoyed Robert that some drivers at stop junctions seem to want a nod or a hand wave personal invite from the other stopped drivers before they would move on. On principal, he refused to do it.

He was of the mind that drivers who do not take the time to learn the rules of the road are dangerous drivers and tend to cause accidents — not to themselves, ironically enough — but to others, who have to attempt to navigate safely around and about them. So, instead of driving on, he simply stared at the driver, waiting for them to figure out how a four-way stop junction worked. First to stop, first to go; two or more cars stopping at the same time, yield to car on the right. The other driver did not, would not, go. Having waited for what seemed like an interminably long time, Robert finally simply took off.

The first thing Robert noticed as the elevator doors to his office area opened was a huge sentry box and barrier barring his way to his office door. Very surreal looking, almost resembling a lava lamp in the way that the colors of it changed, Robert looked quizzically at Alison. She must know how this thing had gotten there.

"What's this?" he asked a distracted and obviously busy Alison.

"What's what?"

"What's this… Checkpoint Charlie doing outside my office? It's a joke, right?"

"Checkpoint Charlie?" repeated Alison, "what are you talking about?"

"You don't see a…" Before he could finish, a patient in her twenties, Jenny, exited the elevator.

"Jenny's your nine o'clock," said Alison, nonchalantly.

"Sure, but how do I get into my office?" Robert asked, still dumbstruck.

"Hello, Dr. Monro," Jenny greeted cheerfully, "mean traffic out there, huh?"

"Tell me about it," said Robert, still trying to figure out what the deal was here because clearly either Alison didn't see the barrier at all or was playing a mean practical joke. However unlikely that was, it was the preferred theory of choice. The more he considered it, however, the more he realized it must be the former: only he could see the barrier and therefore it really didn't exist.

"Should I go on in?" asked Jenny, herself now wondering what the deal was here.

"If you can get through that, go ahead," said Robert, still not wanting to believe that he alone was seeing things that didn't exist.

With a spring in her step, Jenny walked right through the barrier and into his office. Robert felt a pang of relief as he watched her go. He collected his mail as Alison got beeped on the speakerphone by Dr. Harding:

"Alison, do you have a minute?"

"Right there, Dr. Harding," she replied and left her desk. As she got up, she felt a pain shoot up her leg. Robert noticed her gasp slightly and touch her leg.

"Are you okay?" asked Robert, with concern.

"Yes, I'm fine, thanks," answered Alison. Then she walked stiffly to Dr. Harding's office door.

Completely ignoring the imaginary obstruction, Robert walked toward his office and upon crashing into the barrier hard, he fell back onto the floor. Feeling a mix of shock and anger, Robert took stock of the barrier and watched it change colors to various shades of red. Robert scrambled to his feet. An angry little man in uniform, Gruffy, suddenly appeared in what was now recognizable as a sentry box.

"Can't you see that I'm trying to sleep?" the little chap said.

"Who are you?" asked Robert, incredulously.

"I'm in the uniform," Gruffy said tersely, "I ask the questions. Who are you?"

"I'm Dr. Monro and this is my office. Move this barrier immediately."

"Move it yourself, cabbage face," replied Gruffy, as he turned about in his box.

Wondering exactly when her session was going to begin, Jenny appeared in the office doorway.

"I need to get out of here on time today, Dr. Monro," she said, hoping to instill a sense of urgency.

"Jenny, make yourself comfortable. I'll be right with you," said Robert in a more confident tone than belied the uncertainty that he was feeling inside. As Jenny returned to the office, Robert determined to climb over the obstruction. Not as agile as he thought he was, he slipped and fell.

"How come I'm the only one to see this," he asked Gruffy as he scrambled to get up.

"Because it's your barrier, of course," replied Gruffy, matter-of-factly.

"My barrier? I don't remember ordering this?"

"I didn't order the wart on my nose, either," said Gruffy, dismissively.

"You okay, Dr. Monro?" asked Alison as she returned to her desk.

"Yeah," said Robert, trying to look as nonchalant as possible, "just trying out a new technique."

"What's it called? Avoidance therapy?" said Alison with a smile.

"Something like that," replied Robert, still wondering what to do. She stared at him.

"What?" he then asked her as she stood observing what she considered more of his typical weirdness.

"You are the weirdest man that I know," she said, returning to her work.

Again, Jenny appeared at his office doorway, her patience now eroded to zip. Robert didn't give her a chance to speak.

"I'm trying something new today, Jenny," he said, making it up as he went along, "why don't we take the session to the coffee place around the corner?"

Although puzzled, Jenny decided to go along. "Okay," she said, uncertainly.

Robert led the way and Jenny, purse in hand, followed. In the coffee shop, Jenny sat uncomfortably while Robert returned with coffee for each of them. Several thoughts flitted through Jenny's head at once. How intimate could their therapy session get with people all around, chatting to each other and some of them on their cell phones? Suppose she felt like she needed to cry, like in their last session, where she'd had a minor breakthrough? What if someone she knew came in? Why was Dr. Monro taking her for coffee? Holy crap, was he thinking of hitting on her?

"You're not going to make a pass at me, Dr. Monro, are you?" she blurted out as soon as he sat down, "my life is complicated enough..." He stared at her, dumbfounded.

"No, no, of course not," he interrupted. "I needed to get out... I think this is going to work much better... for what we need to talk about," he stumbled.

"Which is?" asked Jenny, unconvinced.

Thump! The earth suddenly shook, causing ripples on Robert's coffee. Thump! Something whacked again, as Robert, frightened, looked around for its source.

"Everything okay?" asked Jenny, wondering what was up with her shrink.

Realizing that he, again, was perhaps the only person to notice, he felt yet another two thumps. "You feel that?" he asked, beginning to panic.

"Feel what?"

Thump! Thump! Thump! Thump! It was the same earth shattering sounds and vibrations that he had observed in his bad dream, he quickly realized. Uncontrollably, his heart started pumping faster. The intense whumping thump occurred again.

"There. You felt that, didn't you?" he asked.

"You mean like an earthquake?"

"Yes," he said, hopefully.

"No. I don't think so," said Jenny, despite her senses being on high alert.

Thump! Thump! Thump! Thump!

"They're getting closer," Robert said, completely panicked, "run for your life!" As if some primal survival instinct had completely taken him over, Robert leapt up and bolted for the door. Jenny looked all around but could perceive no threat. Quizzically, she watched him run down the street in a panic.

Robert pumped his legs as hard and as fast as they could go but it did not seem fast enough. He could still hear the whumping thump of the monster's giant footsteps and the sounds of heavy rasping breathing get closer. Like a man possessed, he ran without thought or strategy. As someone left a store, Robert raced through the closing door, hoping to find safety. He looked around to see that he was now inside of a large book store. There were many shelves full of volumes, behind which he could hide. Tucking down low, between two book shelves, he fell to the floor and breathed as deeply as possible to fill his spent lungs with air. Without daring to risk being seen, he backed up to where the book shelf met the wall and listened intently for any sign of the advancing beast. All was silent.

Relieved beyond reason, he began to feel normal again. The few curious customers that had seen him dash in, now returned to their book browsing. Right before him, on the opposite book shelf, a book cover caught his eye. Below a picture of his patient Miss Blessing, was a book with the title, *Life Is But a Dream*. Miss Blessing has a book in print? he thought to himself.

Life indeed was very strange. Taking down the book, he then remembered taking a potion from her, some supposedly innocent cure for a headache. He tried to remember if it was after taking the powdered remedy that he began seeing and hearing things that didn't exist. What on earth did she give him? he wondered. Then and there he decided to call Alison and get Miss Blessing's home address. Without invite or warning, he was going to pay Miss Blessing a visit and get to the bottom of all the madness he had been experiencing.

Dreams are often most profound when they seem the most crazy.

~Sigmund Freud

A short while later Robert was in a residential area. When he pressed Miss Blessing's doorbell it played what sounded to him like a very silly ditty, something akin to a jingle. It was disturbing and not at all the way a doorbell should sound. A middle-aged man, whom Robert didn't recognize, opened the door. There was something goofy-looking about the man, Robert felt, although he couldn't put his finger upon just what.

"Hello," said the man.

"I'm looking for Miss Blessing… Marjorie Blessing," said Robert.

"Are you one of her fans?" inquired the man, with a somber expression. What a strange question, Robert thought to himself, Miss Blessing has fans?

"I'm her therapist, Dr. Monro," clarified Robert, "she may have mentioned me."

As the man appeared to think hard about the question, Robert spoke again.

"Are you her husband?"

"No, no, not at all. I'm Tom. I'm her brother."

"Pleased to meet you," said Robert, after an awkward pause, "can you tell her that I'm here? It's urgent."

"What's the password?" asked Tom, earnestly. Robert expected Tom to smile like it was a poor joke and then open the door. Instead, he kept his serious facial expression, as if waiting for an answer.

"The password?" repeated Robert, as if it was the most ludicrous thing he ever heard, "what is this, grade school?" As Tom began to close the door, a shocked Robert jammed it open with his foot.

"Life is but a dream," he quickly blurted out, the first thing that came into his head. Tom opened the door so that Robert could enter.

"That was the password?" asked Robert.

"You weren't even close," said Tom and gave him a huge wink.

And people think I'm weird, Robert reflected to himself.

"Robert, what a surprise!" said Miss Blessing, greeting him in the hall. "I see you've met my brother, Tom." Robert's eyes couldn't help but look around; the place was like a mini Xanadu with tchotchkes, antiques, some of which looked like toys of a bygone era and Daliesque artworks.

"We need to talk," said Robert, remembering why he came.

"You're just in time for tea," she said, leading him into another room. Robert followed her and saw that a group of guests were already seated around the table eating what appeared to be cake and cookies and also drinking tea. If he was being generous, he would have described them as colorful, creative types, which in his lexicon were really just code words for crazy and eccentric. Perhaps she misunderstood the nature of his visit, he considered, so he inched closer to whisper in her ear.

"I really need to have a word with you," he said with as urgent a tone as he could muster, "alone." Miss Blessing nodded, as if she were in full agreement, "but first, have some tea." Before Robert had a chance to decline, Miss Blessing stood up.

"Everyone," she said, addressing the assembled, "I'm pleased to announce the arrival of a very talented author and therapist extraordinaire, Dr. Robert Monro." As the guests ad-libbed their greetings, Robert reluctantly sat in a vacant seat that Miss Blessing was directing him to.

"Would we be familiar with any of your books, Dr. Morris?" asked one of the guests.

"Monro, Dr. Monro," Robert corrected, "no, I doubt if you've heard of my books. They're very... specialized."

"We're avid readers," insisted another guest, "please try us."

Robert looked around at all the quiet and expectant faces.

"*Freud's Interpretation Of Dreams, A Critique*?" said Robert to the room of blank faces. "*Dreams And The Psychoanalytical Method*?" he continued, again to a silent reaction among the guests. "How about, *Dream Symbolism and the Study of Hysteria*?" said Robert, again inspiring zero recognition among the assembled, "that one was selected as a top ten book of the decade on subjective analysis of dreams and altered states of consciousness in last year's Journal of Psychiatry," Robert added, proudly, as he always did when mentioning that particular book.

"He also wrote the foreword to the *Complete Moron's Guide to Dream Interpretation*," contributed Miss Blessing, which to his dismay aroused an immediate burst of recognition among the peculiar group.

"Hilarious book," said a guest, more in admiration than as a criticism.

"Best laugh I've had in years," added another, admiringly.

"My publisher wanted me to branch out..." Robert said apologetically but didn't finish.

47

"I mention you in my book, you know," said Miss Blessing as she placed a tea cup and small plate before him, "you've been such an inspiration to my work, Robert."

"You must know so much," a guest said with obvious admiration.

"Lately, I feel like I don't know anything, anymore," Robert confessed.

"That's wonderful," said another guest, perhaps not hearing him correctly.

"What do you mean, Dr. Morris?" asked the first guest.

"I feel like I'm in a dream that I don't know how to wake up from. A bit like *Alice In Wonderland*, I guess," Robert added, pensively. Surprisingly, there was little recognition among the guests to his reference. "Alice fell down a rabbit hole. Ended up at a Madhatter's tea party?"

"Did you end up at a Madhatter's tea party?" asked Tom, earnestly.

"Some tea, Robert?" asked Miss Blessing, pouring already.

"I did fall down through my floorboards," continued Robert.

"You should get that fixed," said a guest.

As if remembering the urgency of his situation, Robert stood.

"You know, you're right," he said as if waking from a stupor, "if you'll excuse me, I have to leave." The guests expressed their disappointment.

"We were hoping you might share some nuggets of wisdom with us, Dr. Morrow," said the first guest.

"Monro. Dr. Monro," corrected Robert, now feeling frazzled and annoyed.

Miss Blessing caught up with him in the front room. "I'm so sorry you have to…"

"What did you put in my water?" he interrupted sharply, "that stuff… that powder?"

"What's happening?" Miss Blessing asked with great interest, "are you seeing things?"

"Seeing things?!" repeated Robert, almost shouting. "My world is turned upside down. I don't know what's real and what's a dream. I don't know if I'm in a dream, right now."

"That's terrific," exclaimed Miss Blessing, with obvious pleasure.

"What's terrific about it? My wife's left me; my father's in a coma; I'm locked out of my office by some... cartoon character. I'm going out of my mind. Maybe I will wake up and realize that it was all a very bad dream," Robert continued, feeling fear increasingly creep into his consciousness, "but what if I never wake up?"

"This is all so exciting," exclaimed Miss Blessing.

"What?" asked Robert, wondering if she is listening or has simply lost her mind.

"Aren't you the dream expert?" she asked, in a more serious tone, "I mean, you were so helpful to me when I was going through something similar... Isn't dream interpretation your whole bailiwick?"

"It is my specialty, yes," answered Robert, wondering what point she was making.

"And here you are, in what must be the biggest adventure of your life... Or is it all just theory, with you?"

Robert thought somberly about her question. Like her or not, she did hit a nerve with her questioning and particularly her use of the word, "theory." He couldn't remember the last time he was challenged like this by a peer in his field, let alone an outsider, a client, for crying out loud.

"I need to solve the puzzle of my own dreams? Is that what you're suggesting?" he asked, knowing that that was precisely what she meant and, of course, it was exactly what he must do.

"You're very brilliant up here," said Miss Blessing, tenderly touching his head, "but you've forgotten that it's down here that holds all the answers," she said and touched his heart.

"I came here hoping that you'd have some way of stopping all this, maybe have some antidote for that stuff that I foolishly took," Robert said.

"You told me once that the only way to end a bad dream was to wake from it. You also said that once you do, you'll be deeply rewarded by the experience," Miss Blessing said softly. "Perhaps these were not your actual words but you do remember and understand the sentiment, yes? You said that waking from the dream would transform me entirely and be positive in ways that I could not imagine."

Feeling suddenly very tired and somewhat defeated, Robert turned to go on his way.

"Wait. I have something for you," Miss Blessing said and then she took a framed print from the wall and gave it to him. It was a print of St. George killing the dragon, the exact same image which he gives to all of his clients, except this one was mounted in a golden frame. He looked at the image, almost tearfully.

"As a brilliant man once told me," she almost whispered, "stop running, turn around, and take charge." His own words, repeated back to him, were for some reason quite hard to take. He was in no mood to analyze why or indeed analyze anything, for that matter. He felt like leaving, getting to his house, and crawling into bed.

"Like you were here for me, Robert, I'm here for you... at any time."

Robert managed to nod in acknowledgment when all that he wanted to do was go home immediately and be alone. He took the print and left. When he got into his car, and remembered that he would be returning to an empty house, he was filled with waves of despair. He didn't want to be alone; he wanted to be with his wife and son. He wanted to walk in the front door and be greeted warmly and receive a kiss from Gail and a hug from Jason. He wanted to be excited about returning to a home filled with the smells of fresh baked goodness, shared warmth and love of his family. He hoped that they would be back home. Considering how his reality was all messed up, perhaps they were at home right now, Gail cooking dinner and Jason playing a video game.

He felt himself get excited. Not wanting to get totally bummed out when he got home and they were not there, he decided he'd call Gail's cell.

"Hi, thanks for calling. Meg, Gail and Jason have gone on a cruise, lucky us. Leave a message if it's important and I'll get back to you…"

Robert hung up, and felt a surge of intense anger. What a selfish bitch, he cursed to himself.

In sleep, fantasy takes the form of dreams. But in waking life, too, we continue to dream beneath the threshold of consciousness, especially when under the influence of repressed or other unconscious complexes.

~Carl Jung

Gail looked terrific, in a borrowed evening dress, as she left the crowded ballroom floor and walked out onto the ship's deck to get some fresh sea air. Fumbling in her evening bag for her lipstick, she instead found a tiny old bottle of prescription pills. She looked at it as if it jogged her memory to another time and place. I was a different person when I relied on these to get through the day, she mused. Well, guess what? she said to herself. A couple of days on a cruise, away from the monotony of her home life and she felt great. I don't need these things anymore; perhaps I never did. She threw the bottle overboard with a wild sense of freedom and deep satisfaction.

"He's cute," Meg said as she joined her from the ballroom, "and totally into you."

"Who is?" questioned Gail, knowing full well who her sister was referring to.

"The guy you've been dancing with all night." Meg giggled and it reminded Gail of when they were teenagers gabbing about boys and dates and true love.

"Three dances isn't all night. He asked me to dance, what was I going to say, no?" said Gail, secretly pleased with herself that a handsome young man would still find her attractive.

"What were you littering the ocean with?" asked Meg. Feeling secretive, Gail remained silent. She definitely did not want the conversation to go there. "It looked like your prescription pills. Was the bottle empty?" continued Meg, trying to lure her into revealing what she was up to.

"Thanks to you, this cruise is the only medicine that I need," said Gail, hoping to deflect her persistent sister with a compliment. Meg laughed.

"No. Being away from your sourpuss husband is the only medication you need."

"He wasn't always like that, Meg."

"He doesn't make you happy, Gail," said Meg veering into heavy talk.

"We went on a cruise for our honeymoon," announced Gail with a cheerful smile. "I remember we entered this dancing competition, but neither of us were dancers… we just made it all up as we went along. You should have seen him, he was seriously goofy!" As Gail remembered more of the event, it made her laugh a bit and smile even more.

"That's what I've been telling you, the guy *is* goofy," said Meg, feeling vindicated.

"I mean, acting goofy," corrected Gail, "not goofy as a character trait, although he probably is a little guilty of being that too," she added, wistfully.

The scene in question, now uploaded into Gail's present consciousness, started to play and Gail decided to watch it rather than dismiss it and change her thoughts to something. In her mind's eye there was a smaller ballroom than the one she had just left. There were but two dancing couples remaining on the dance floor: she and Robert and an elegant, older couple, who really could dance. Each dancer had a number pinned to their backs. Contrary to her and Robert, who were laughing their heads off, the other couple were serious and seemed quite intent upon winning.

"Cindy and Brad, you guys have style," she remembered the DJ saying, as the crowd applauded. "Gail and Robert, I haven't seen anyone move like that since the Three Stooges went to funky town," the DJ said, trying especially hard to be off-the-cuff funny. In her memory, Robert and she were the audience favorites, as the audience laughed uproariously every time either of them did a funny dance move.

"Ladies and gentlemen," announced the DJ, "in a fair world, Cindy and Brad would win the prize for a wonderful display of grace and elegance. But for sheer laugh out loud lunacy, I'm awarding first place to Gail and Robert! Give them a big hand."

As the audience gave them a stirring round of applause, Robert swept Gail up into his arms and twirled her around. In his head, I'm sure he thought he was being graceful, she considered, but in reality, he was as clumsy as all get out and almost tripped and fell on top of her. They pranced around with their first prize, a large golden cup, and laughed and laughed as the audience cheered them on.

"I wish you had known him, back then," said Gail to her sister, still smiling over her memories.

"Well, that was then. This is now," replied Meg, not privy to the feel-good warmth her sister seemed to be feeling. "Well, if you don't want Mr. Handsome Young

Stud, my dance card has a couple of openings," said Meg, half winking. Then she returned to the ballroom.

Gail remained on deck. She felt terrifically energized and appreciative of everything in her view: the sparkling ocean, crescent moon and its multifaceted reflections, the life-restoring sea air and the amazing behemoth of a luxury vessel. She reveled in the magic that allowed this great thing with its size and its heft to defy reality and skim the surface of the wild, wind-swept sea, so that hundreds of people could dance and play on the untamed ocean.

Dreams are true while they last, and do we not live in dreams?

~Alfred Lord Tennyson

After heating up an unappetizing frozen dinner, Robert took his coffee into the office. He thought that he would use this time to catch up on an increasingly large pile of unread Psychiatry Today magazines. All alone in the empty house, he felt like a loose screw in a tin box which rattles around when shaken. He was feeling so restless, he could not stay still. He decided that he must become more proactive about his situation, not to be so resigned to his fate.

What if that barrier continues blocking his office indefinitely? He had canceled far too many client sessions in a short space of time. It must not continue. Above all else, holding onto his office and practice was a top priority. Getting an idea, he left the house through the back door. He walked across the back yard and unlocked and entered the garden shed.

Wheeling around a beat up, rusting wheelbarrow, he filled it with all of the heavy-duty equipment he could find in the shed, objects he had forgotten about or didn't even know he had. There was a chain saw, an acetylene torch, and a hatchet and other he-man guy tools. He loaded all of it into

Gail's Volvo station wagon, the wheelbarrow included, and then drove off.

A short time later, Robert was pushing the wheelbarrow full of heavy-duty tools down a city street. Stopping outside his office building, he tapped on the glass to get the attention of Frank, the night security guard. As Frank opened the door, Robert trundled the wheelbarrow on through.

"Evening, Frank," said Robert, very casually.

"Working late, Dr. Monro?" Frank asked, looking at all of the psychiatrist's crazy gear, hoping for more than the typical greeting.

"Yeah, got some odd jobs to do in the office," said Robert, wasting no time in getting his load to the elevator.

"It's not something that the maintenance guys can handle, Dr. Monro?" asked Frank, wondering if everything was above board. He couldn't help but worry that this was something that was going to get him into trouble.

"No, I'm good," said Robert, calmly, as the elevator doors closed with a ding.

Once the elevator got to his floor, Robert patted himself on the back. The barrier was indeed still blocking entry to his office. He wheeled the collection of heavy duty tools over to the barrier and considered which would be the most appropriate tool to start with. Deciding to go with the acetylene torch, he struck a match, lit the gas and adjusted the noisy flame to a small blue orange jet of fire. Gruffy awoke and popped his head up over the sentry box.

"What's all the noise?" he asked testily.

"No more Mr. Nice Guy," Robert said, donning a protective mask.

"This oughta be good," Gruffy said, unconvinced.

When Robert set the torch against the barrier, sparks began to fly. Soon there was a shower of glowing embers that sparkled and glowed as they flew through the air. The barrier was made of a metal that he was unfamiliar with but, considering he was never much of a handyman, that didn't mean very much. With the flame of the torch against it, the barrier color grew darker and darker and soon turned to black.

Beginning to really wonder what Dr. Monro was up to, from his security desk downstairs, Frank threw some switches on his CCTV. Then he clicked through a series of surveillance camera shots; empty hallways and offices until he landed upon camera footage of Robert outside his office door. Frank watched with interest, trying to make out what Dr. Monro was doing exactly. It appeared that he was using a heavy duty torch to cut through his own office door. Knowing that he had better cover his own ass, Frank decided the best person to call would be Dr. Harding.

After a bit, Robert put out the torch and surveyed the state of the barrier. To his amazement, the metal was not at all damaged. Its colors had turned to browns and greens.

"That was pretty dumb, Banana Face," said Gruffy, snidely.

"It didn't even put a mark on it?" said Robert, half making a statement, half questioning. Gruffy grunted in response. "What kind of metal is this?" Robert asked.

"It's Shakespearean metal," replied Gruffy, in a superior tone.

"Shakespearean metal?"

"Yeah," responded Gruffy, "it's made of the same stuff that dreams are made of."

"Not to be outdone or discouraged, Robert revved up a chainsaw. "We'll see about that," he said with resolve and again attacked the barrier. Gruffy inspected his finger nails as he patiently waited for Robert to be finished. Even though sparks were flying, the chainsaw didn't seem to be having any effect, whatsoever. Robert turned it off and inspected his latest effort, again not a scratch.

"I don't get it," he said, now so annoyed that he kicked the barrier, "okay, tell me how to get rid of this thing!"

"You're not going to get rid of it if you're not going to be nice to it," Gruffy responded cryptically.

"Nice?" said Robert, almost in a shout, "you want me to be nice? I'll show you nice!"

Attacking the barrier with a hatchet, he let it have all the anger that had built up inside him of the last couple of weeks. To make matters worse, Gruffy cheered him on.

Robert stopped, more from exhaustion than from making any progress. He was again astounded that there was not a scratch on the barrier.

"You're not so big and powerful, after all, are you now, Skinny Puss?" jeered Gruffy.

"Call me one more stupid, infantile name…" said Robert, breathlessly. Watching the swirling mass of colors of the barrier, twist and change, Robert got an idea.

"You no good son of a bitch, mean-ass, messed up in the head barrier!" he yelled at the barrier. He then smiled as he watched the colors darken towards black. It's like a mood ring, he thought to himself. Very sweetly, he began to compliment and sweet-talk the barrier.

"What a lovely, charming, beautiful, and generous little barrier you are," he cooed. The barrier became lighter in color.

"That's it, isn't it?" he questioned Gruffy, "it's only a barrier if I'm angry, right?"

"You don't know what you're talking about, Dr. Quack."

"Oh, yeah?" Robert said confidently and again addressed the barrier, "I love you, you sweet little thing." The barrier turned bright pink in color, as if it were blushing.

"You don't mean a word, you phony excuse for a man. You never loved anyone in your life, not even yourself," countered Gruffy, his tone of voice indicating that he felt somewhat threatened. Robert then stroked the barrier, as if it were an adored pet.

"Oh, you feel real good. How did you get such a soft and silky exterior? I think I'm falling in love with you," said Robert, really getting into it. The barrier turned more and more translucent as Robert continued to say complimentary and loving things to it.

Downstairs at the security desk, Frank and Dr. Harding watched Robert, with interest. On the small screen, Robert looked like he was stooping down and petting and talking to his office door. He resembled a schizophrenic lost in his own world.

"You can't get audio on this thing?" asked Dr. Harding.

"No, sir. Just visual."

"Let's go up," said Harding, "and bring your weapon, this could get ugly."

Frank did a mental double-take, wondering exactly what Harding meant by "bring your weapon." He didn't carry a firearm, if that's what the doc was implying. He did have a small billy stick, but what kind of ugly was Harding expecting? Monro didn't seem like the crazy, I'm-going-to-hurt-you kind. Besides, Frank thought, the guy's not so big that he couldn't be taken down pretty easily. Harding's been watching too much TV, Frank concluded. All of these docs seem a little kooky. This isn't "Die Hard," after all.

Robert exuded so much love to the barrier that it began to fade, so much so, that he could now walk effortlessly through the thing. Both the sentry box and Gruffy himself, were fading along with it.

"Coochy, coochy, coochy, coo…" continued Robert, loving every moment. Mad as hell, Gruffy was getting more and more faint.

"You wouldn't know love if it jumped up and bit your ugly, miserable excuse for a nose," he said weakly, not giving up the fight, "you dumb-ass imposter!"

The barrier, sentry box and Gruffy faded completely from view as the elevator doors opened. Smiling broadly,

Robert turned to see Harding and Frank walk toward him purposefully.

"Do you mind explaining exactly what's going on around here?" asked Harding, checking out Robert's wheelbarrow of tools and expecting to see some property damage.

"The door hinges needed some oil," said Robert, not caring at all how things might appear. "I handled it, though. You two have a terrific evening," he added, then wheeled the barrow towards the elevator. Unable to see any damage or find any reason to stop him, Harding felt that at least, he should issue some kind of warning to the guy.

"You're hanging on by a thin thread around here, Monro. Hanging on by a thread," he said, repeating himself for greater emphasis.

As the elevator doors closed on Robert, Harding again took a look around for any signs of mischief. Unable to find any, he turned to Frank who was as baffled-looking.

"Keep a close eye on him for me, will you, Frank?" Harding finally said, more to save face than as an actual command.

"You bet, sir," answered Frank, hoping that the entire embarrassing episode was over so that he could get back to his desk and his portable TV.

Once he reached the ground floor, Robert wheeled the barrow out of the elevator, out the rear door and directly into the parking lot. As he approached the station wagon, he stopped abruptly and listened. Was that a sound? Sure enough, he wasn't imagining it.

Thump! Thump! Thump! Thump! Thump! The combination of hellish breathing and gigantic footsteps put Robert into immediate panic mode. As the footsteps got closer, his feet involuntarily ran like crazy. As he became aware of what was happening, he realized that he was still pushing the wheelbarrow. Quickly ditching it, he picked up the pace.

The thumping of the approaching monsters, dragons, or whatever they were, got closer and louder. He ran through the quiet streets, faster and faster, and tried to mentally overcome his fear. Stop running, turn around, take charge, he managed to say to himself. Then he repeated the phrases with more and more belief and greater intensity.

"Stop running! Turn around! Take charge!" he shouted out loud to himself, willing himself to have courage until finally, with all the spunk he could muster, he decided to stop and turn around. He braced himself for the worst. Stopping quickly and turning, he lost his balance and fell to the ground. He let out an involuntary scream and automatically assumed a protective position, covering his head and face with his arms.

The footsteps and the heavy breathing of the monsters stopped but, with his eyes shut tight, Robert couldn't tell if they were near or far or still there at all. Fearfully, he slowly opened his eyes to a squint. Two harmless looking little boys stood before him. One was aged ten or so and the other was maybe six years old. Robert looked around them and behind them but could see no other threat. He sat up straighter to get a closer look at the two boys. Sharing a physical resemblance with him, they could easily pass for his sons.

"You're the dragons?" asked Robert, incredulously. The two boys exchanged a glance, obviously puzzled by his question. "What do you want?" questioned Robert. He got up off of the ground. Again, the boys reacted in a confused and puzzled manner.

"Why have you been chasing me?" Robert continued, wondering now if they were a pair of mutes.

"We've always been chasing you," the older one said.

"Why did you stop?" asked the younger boy, just as confused as his slightly older companion.

"You've always been chasing me?" asked Robert, trying to solve the puzzle, "since when?" The boys looked to each other, they obviously didn't know, either.

"Are you taking us home?" the younger boy asked hopefully.

"You guys had me terrified out of my wits," said Robert, still in shock, "how did you learn to make so much noise?"

"Are you going to take us home, now?" the older boy asked with excitement.

"Take you guys home?" repeated Robert, his brain seemingly working slowly, "I've already got a son." The two boys dropped their heads in abject disappointment.

"He's about your age," Robert said to the older one, "how old are you, about ten?"

Too upset to respond, the older boy looked at his own shoes. Feeling bad for the boys and more chipper than he'd felt in some time, Robert decided that he would indeed take the boys home and figure out where to take things from there. Besides, he considered, it was lonely at home without Gail and Jason.

"I think you'd like him, when you meet him," said Robert, smiling. The boys immediately brightened up.

"You're taking us home?" the younger one asked, grinning from ear to ear.

"Sure," smiled Robert, "why not?" The two boys jumped and danced with joy.

"Let's get some ice cream," suggested Robert, buoyed by their obvious delight, "you guys like ice cream?" The boys almost lost their minds with excitement. They skipped and danced beside Robert as he walked them back to his car.

"What are your names?" asked Robert. Bewildered by the question, it was clear to him that the boys obviously didn't know. "You don't have names?" said Robert.

"Nobody ever talks to us. They don't even know we're here," said the oldest child.

"We're just lost," said the younger boy, sadly.

"You're the lost boys," said Robert, dredging his mental knowledge base, "my lost boys."

61

Robert felt far more optimistic about his situation as he drove the kids back to his house. Looking in the mirror, he briefly watched as the two boys licked their ice cream cones with ravenous delight. I've slain my dragons, he thought to himself; dragons that turned out to be two harmless and adorable little children. He wanted to tell someone, talk to a sympathetic ear about his process, how he was cracking the puzzle to his own life, his own dream... but who? Gail was incommunicado; Professor Heathcliff already thought he was bonkers. So he called Miss Blessing.

"Marjorie Blessing speaking," Miss Blessing answered warmly.

"Marjorie, it's Robert."

"Yes, Robert."

"I'm calling you... well, frankly, I don't have anyone else I can call," Robert said honestly, if not a little apologetically, "I'm figuring it all out, just as you told me I should, same way I analyze dreams with my clients."

"That's terrific, Robert," Miss Blessing said, brightly.

"These imaginary people I keep seeing? You're right. They all represent something, some aspect of my psyche that I have needed to pay attention to, some lost parts of myself that have been seeking integration and healing. It's incredible." He paused, entirely excited and grateful.

"Yes, Robert," said Miss Blessing, like a good therapist, being non-committal but encouraging, all the same. He took a deep breath and continued.

"That barrier preventing me from getting into my office?" he continued, "it was my anger. And get this," he said more energized by the moment, "the 'dragons' that kept chasing me? Turns out they're two lovable little kids, my own inner children, who just happen to love attention and ice cream and have been lost all this time. I figure that they represent me when I was younger. They must have experienced trauma of some kind and split off from me, the trauma arresting their development. If I can reintegrate them, I'm healed!" He gave Miss Blessing a chance to comment.

"I'm so happy for you, Robert. You know that you can call on me any time you want to bounce ideas around but it sounds like you've got some real clarity on this,"

"I do… and I appreciate that, Marjorie," replied Robert, feeling better than he had felt in an age, "but you know what? I think this is it, game over. I've faced my dragons, I'm healing my inner torment and I feel like a million bucks. Let's get together, sometime."

"I would like that very much," said Miss Blessing, and managed to hide her doubt. When she hung up the phone, Tom, who was sitting across the checkers board from her, asked her what was wrong.

"That was Robert," she said, "he's doing fine but I think he may be overlooking a very significant defect in his shadow personality."

"What's that, Marge?" asked Tom with curiosity.

"Arrogance, Tom," Miss Blessing said with concern, "arrogance."

When Robert pulled into his driveway, he turned and announced their arrival.

"We're home, boys!" The boys were both ecstatic and they reached over the driver's seat to hug him simultaneously.

"Thank you, thank you, thank you…" they both chanted, "we love you so much."

They hugged Robert so tight and with such great love, and said their feelings so lovingly, that it brought tears to his eyes.

"Well, you're welcome," he blurted. Then he got out of the car and opened the rear door to let the boys out. When he didn't see their happy smiling selves exiting the car, he looked in to see what the hold up was.

His heart practically stopped when he saw that there was nothing but an empty vehicle interior. It was as if they had vanished into thin air not leaving a trace behind. Did they reintegrate into his psyche or is this yet another trick of the mind, he wondered? Did he imagine them? What if he had a tumor on his brain? Everything he had been experiencing of late would be consistent with the symptoms associated with having a brain tumor. Wait, maybe it was schizophrenia?

As he entered his house, he resolved to have his brain checked out. He would get a brain scan, an MRI, or whatever else he needed, just to be on the safe side and assemble some facts. Why didn't I think of this much earlier, he asked himself? Is it just my training that makes me conclude that whatever is going on with me can be explained by the mind? Why do I always think that it's psychological and nothing else? Of course it could be physical, a brain tumor or maybe even early Parkinson's.

Just thinking about the terrible possibilities made Robert weak at the knees. In truth, he didn't want to consider that he might have anything other than a healthy mind and body. Suppose he did have inoperable cancer in the brain? What then? How could he live with that? Plain and simple, he couldn't. He knew himself well enough to know that brain cancer was something that he couldn't handle, at all. If he did have something fatal, he was better off not knowing. Let me live my life as normally as I can and, some innocuous evening, the cancer can take me in my sleep. Game over. What he really wanted was to go to bed and wake up with his life back to normal. Normal, normal, normal, he repeated to himself, as if saying it often enough would force it to be so.

A dream which is not interpreted is like a letter which is not read.

~The Talmud

The next day started normally enough. Up at the right time, he got something to eat, had a cup of coffee and was in the car on time. Coming to the all-way stop intersection, the same players assembled for their morning routine. There was the bad driver on his right, chronically indecisive; the other drivers, impatient, unwilling to come to a complete stop adding to the danger and anger of the moment. Deciding that today, he was simply going to wait, Robert applauded the bad driver as she drove hesitantly into the intersection.

"There you go, you can do it," he said to her as he watched her go.

As the elevator doors opened to reveal his office, Robert balked at the sight of the barrier and sentry box, blocking his office, once again. Wondering why it would have returned, he questioned himself about whether, after blow torching it, he actually did love it to death the previous evening. Or was that a dream? Alison greeted him a good morning, as she walked with some obvious pain into Dr. Harding's office.

"You wanted to see me, Dr. Harding," Robert heard her say.

"Yes, Alison. Take a seat."

Inside Dr. Harding's office, Alison sat down and appeared to be in some pain.

"You're not planning on taking another sick day, are you?" Dr. Harding asked. "You've pretty much used up those and are well into your vacation days, at this point."

Considering the inordinate number of days she had called in sick, Alison knew that Harding was maybe one more sick day away from firing her. In fact, he had warned her of that fact a while ago, although she was not sure if it was a threat he would actually carry out.

In the reception area, annoyed as hell, Robert kicked the sentry box and woke Gruffy up.

"Who goes there?" snapped Gruffy.

"I thought I got rid of you?" questioned Robert.

"Apparently not," said Gruffy.

Through the open door, from inside Harding's office, Alison could see that Robert was acting strange and possibly talking to himself again.

"What's going on out there?" Harding asked, noticing her obvious distraction.

"Dr. Monro just came in," she replied, "I've got some phone messages for him."

"How has Dr. Monro been behaving lately?" he asked in a confidential tone, "Have you noticed anything strange?"

Alison quickly glanced out to see Robert kicking at something that she couldn't see.

"He's a very experimental therapist," Alison said, "he does try out different techniques, and stuff."

"He has also canceled a lot of appointments lately…" Harding said, checking his log book. Alison again looked out front and saw, what looked like, Robert choking an imaginary person. "He's had some personal issues," Alison said, distracted, "his father…"

"Yes," interrupted Harding, "I heard his father was ill… what are you looking at?"

Harding looked like he might get up and investigate himself to see what was distracting Alison. Alison jumped up from her seat to prevent him from doing so.

"My phone is blinking," she lied, "be right back."

Robert had a good stranglehold on Gruffy's neck as he got all up in Gruffy's face.

"I've had it with you and this piece of crap! You're ruining my practice," Robert said.

"Who's ruining your practice?" asked Alison as she made her way to her desk.

"I'm preparing for my nine o'clock, Alison," Robert replied, "I'm role-playing."

"I'd nix the role-playing, if I were you," warned Alison, "Harding's on the war path."

Robert gestured a silent 'thank you' to her as she finished with her desk and then made her way back to Harding's office. A moment later, the elevator doors opened to reveal Robert's nine o'clock appointment, Tony Applegate.

"Mr. Applegate," greeted Robert, "why don't we take our session over coffee at the Coffee Grind downstairs, my treat?"

"Okay," said Tony, uncertainly, "that would be a change, I guess."

"Exactly!" said Robert, reassuringly. Mr. Applegate followed Robert downstairs and, yet again, he tried to fulfill his duties as a therapist in an unconventional setting.

A wave of sadness and despair crept over Robert as he struggled to concentrate upon Applegate's words. They were tucked into a quiet corner of the coffee shop, which was unusually calm, due to the heavy rain that fell outside.

"I'm in a church. It's my wedding and I'm getting married to Wendy, Amy's sister," continued Applegate, in a more subdued tone than usual. "Amy gives her away. But they're both in wedding dresses?" Applegate said. His statement sounded more like a question, "Does that make me a bigamist?"

"Yes…" Robert answered automatically, "in the dream, a bigamist in the dream," he corrected himself. His phone vibrated and he glanced at the caller ID, which said 'unknown.' "I should take this," Robert said apologetically, "it could be about my father. He's ill."

"Sure, of course," said Applegate, understandingly.

"Hello?" Robert spoke into the phone.

"It's Gail," said a voice that sounded weak and distant.

"Where are you?" asked Robert, shocked, yet excited.

"Some small port in Mexico, just for a few hours."

"When are you coming home? I miss you," said Robert, feeling totally disconnected from his wife.

"We took a cruise with Meg. Jason is having a blast," said Gail. The line was so bad, he wondered if she could hear him clearly. "I'm sorry I haven't called sooner, I…" Gail either paused or the line broke up but Robert wondered if she was perhaps a little tearful. True or not, it made him feel better. "How are things with you?" he then heard her ask.

"Good. Things are good," answered Robert, afraid at any moment they were going to get cut off, "when are you getting back?"

"I'm not sure of the dates," Gail said, sounding confused, "soon, though. I have to go. Jason says to give you a big hello."

"A big hello back," smiled Robert. He was about to continue but the line went dead. He held the phone to his ear longer than he needed to, perhaps indicating his inner wish to have had a longer connection. Applegate waited for Robert to speak first and hopefully answer some questions that he felt were inappropriate to ask. He couldn't help but wonder if Dr. Monro was having marital problems of his own? Robert stared at his cell phone and Applegate realized that maybe he should speak first and bring Dr. Monro back to the here and now.

"You know, come to think of it, I married Wendy in Mexico," he said. He kept his tone as casual as he could and leafed through his thick dream journal. "Here's my dream journal entry for March 15th of this year," he continued, now reading his notes, "Wendy and I elope to Mexico. She marries me topless."

"Your wife married you… topless in Mexico?" asked Robert, still lost in his own world.

"In a dream," corrected Applegate, "it was a dream I had back in March, remember? We discussed it." Robert didn't remember or wasn't in the frame of mind to try and remember. Sadness and despair took him over, permeating every cell and fiber of his mind and body.

"Will you excuse me for a moment," Robert said. Then he stood and went to the restroom.

Pants fully on, face in his hands, Robert sat on the toilet seat in a stall in the coffee shop restroom. He could not remember a time when he had felt so low, so incapable of helping himself. With his years of training, his expertise, his knowledge, his 'brilliance,' as others had so often remarked, all of his research, writings and publications, all of it seemed worthless to him now. Help me, he heard himself say, to no one in particular.

If I were my own patient, I mean, client, he corrected himself, I would prescribe something for depression. Perhaps I should get some help, he thought, not from Heathcliff or anyone he knows, though. I could show up anonymously at someone else's practice. But then, realistically, what help could they give me that I couldn't give myself?

Why sit across from an inferior therapist and squirm while he or she tries unsuccessfully to analyze the dreams I've been having? If they are hallucinations, they will probably recommend that I commit myself to a facility somewhere for inpatient treatment.

Knowing that he should get up and go, but unable to summon the energy to move, he wondered how he would carry on. Oh, god, please help me, he said to himself again, although he wasn't fully sure that he believed in a god. For the first time in his life, he felt like he knew absolutely nothing. If he had it in himself to laugh at the irony of it all, he would no doubt be in stitches. You spend your life amassing millions, if not zillions, of bits of information and data… only to wake up some rainy day and discover that it was all for naught.

"Talk to your father."

Robert's mind reverie came to an abrupt cessation as he heard words which did not come from his own thoughts. His mind cleared and snapped to attention. He was sure that he had just heard a woman's voice. It sounded like it came from outside but there was no one else in the bathroom. It could only have come from the inside of his own mind, which was a far scarier proposition. Was he starting to hear voices now, as well as see things that didn't exist? Surprisingly, however, he didn't feel all that spooked.

He had a feeling, more of a knowing, actually, that the voice which he had just heard belonged to the Elusive Lady, that mysterious spirit-like entity that seemed to ooze love, and not evil. Like, perhaps, most spirits do, he considered. He was in uncharted territory and feeling very uncertain, as he'd had no prior experience with ghosts. He listened intently for her voice again, or any voice, for that matter. The more that he listened to the silence, the more that he doubted that he had heard a voice in the first place. Oh boy, the mind is a mysterious and complex thing, he concluded.

At least, now, he felt like he could get out and face the world again. He exited the stall. As he washed his hands, at the wash basin, he wondered what significance the message about talking to his father could have for him. As it came from his subconscious mind, it had to mean something. His elementary psychology training could have told him that. But what? His father was in a coma, what kind of conversation could he possibly have with the man? 'Talk to your father,' he mulled over the phrase. 'Talk to' is different than 'talk with,' he considered. The former suggested a conversation and the latter implied more of a one-way communication.

The literature was mixed on the effectiveness of talking to people who lay in a coma, running the gamut from useless to miraculous, depending on which end of the fuzzy, pseudo-psychology spectrum you cared to investigate. But perhaps the benefit would be for himself and not for his father. What do I have to lose, he asked himself, as he left the bathroom.

In dreams the mind is constantly giving you substitutes just to protect sleep. And the same is happening while you are awake. The mind is giving you substitutes just to protect your sanity; otherwise you will be scattered in fragments.

~OSHO

Anita sat by her husband's side as he remained in a coma in intensive care.

"Where on earth have you been?" Anita asked Robert when he arrived.

Surprised by her sense of urgency, he asked, "what's up?"

"He needs a new kidney," Anita said, her voice warbling, "he needs a kidney transplant or he's not going to make it."

"They have a kidney available?" asked Robert, confused, "isn't there a waiting list?"

"Six months, at the earliest," said Anita, getting more tearful. "You two have the same blood type," she said pointedly.

"You want my kidney?" Robert blurted out.

"You'd be saving your father's life," life Anita said, puzzled by his reaction, "don't you want to give him one of your kidneys?"

"Relax, mother," Robert said, calming himself down, "you just sprung this on me. Of course I'll give him one of my kidneys. If that's what it takes, sure." Robert wasn't sure. He had surprised himself with his first reaction to her mother's news. It would seem like a given, a slam dunk, that a loving son would give up a kidney to save his own father's life. Yet, he was balking inside. Why? Is that a natural reaction to the possible loss of a kidney, he thought? Or is there something deeper than that going on? Would he really begrudge his father one of his healthy kidneys? Robert suddenly craved some coffee, any coffee.

"I'm going to get some coffee from the vending machine," he told his mom, "you want some?"

"If I drink any more coffee, we'd need both of your kidneys," answered Anita, surprising them both, as she was not known for her off-the-cuff humor.

"That's funny," said Robert, not amused. "I'll be right back."

As he left the intensive care unit, he heaved a couple of deep breaths. Leaving to get coffee from the vending machine allowed him some time to calm down and adjust to the reality of his father's situation. When he returned to his mother, Anita behaved as if she were seeing him for the first time today.

"You look terrible," she said, "did you sleep in that suit?" Robert was now focused on his awareness that he needed time alone to 'talk with his father.'

"Mom, can you give us a few minutes?" he asked "I want to talk to father."

"Your father's in a coma," Anita said, puzzled, "what do you think he's going to say?"

"It's good to talk to a person in a coma," he answered authoritatively.

"Well, if you get him to talk, ask him where he left his new will. I can't find it anywhere."

"I'll ask," said Robert, and held open the room door. Robert waited, silently standing by his father's bed until a nurse finished recording some readings from the life support machines and left. Robert had great difficulty deciding what to say to his sleeping old man.

"Father," he started, tentatively, "dad… look, I know we haven't spoken meaningfully to each other in…"
Listening to himself talk, he felt so corny and self-conscious. Ready to quit, he walked as far as the door, then stopped. He walked back. He'd try a different tack.

"Okay, here's the thing," he began, "I'm stuck in some kind of dream-like reality. I don't know if I'm in a dream or maybe things are real and I'm seeing things and hearing things or could be I'm sick and I'm just plain losing my mind… Anyway, somehow I've got to get to the source of things, the core issues, and… I think in some way, you might hold the key, maybe you've got some clue I need to solve this puzzle and wake up and get on with my life but, god, I hate your guts!" Robert stood back from the bed, stunned with the words that had just come out of his mouth. 'I hate your guts?!' he repeated to himself; where did that come from?

"Well?" Anita said as she entered, surprising Robert and causing him to jump in surprise. "Did he say anything?" she inquired, a bit flippantly.

"I don't think it did much good," Robert admitted, still reeling from his discovery.

"Tell me about it," said Anita, "I've been talking to him for forty-four years. I don't think that ever did much good, either. Where do you think he's gone?"

"I don't know. Nobody knows. He's probably stuck in a dream somewhere that he can't wake up from," Robert said with irony only he himself would get.

"You'll give him the kidney?" Anita asked, softly.

"Of course," Robert said, and put a comforting arm around his mother. Then they sat and quietly watched the sleeping old man. The next thing he knew, he was waking up in the chair he had sat down in. His mom most likely let him rest and slipped off home. He couldn't see a clock but it felt like it was very late. The ward was deathly quiet, the lights down low; it was probably sometime in the AM, he figured. Feeling very sleepy, he got up and left.

Leaving the hospital to walk to his car, he soon realized that all the parked cars were old, probably made in the sixties. He quickly considered that maybe there was a classic car convention in the morning or a fund-raiser for the hospital or maybe they were making a movie. Then, as he looked around, he was shocked to discover that he was no longer on a city street in modern day Chicago. Incredulous, he turned around and looked behind him. The hospital he just walked out of had a sign that said, 'Pentonville Public Hospital.' Across the way was Jenkins department store; Maurice's Music Store; Clancy's Bar... Somehow he had been transported back to his hometown of Pentonville, Illinois and, judging by the cars, people, stores and fashions, he was back in the sixties again.

As shocking as it was to find himself suddenly in a completely different reality, the recent events that he had experienced, and the fact that he was back in his hometown, on the familiar turf of his childhood, somewhat softened the blow.

Nothing for me to do but follow the latest clue, he thought to himself. Whether I'm at home in bed sleeping, or on the hospital chair still, either way, there's a puzzle to be solved. From now on I'd better trust my instincts instead of trying to reason everything out with my left brain logic. As he walked the familiar city streets, he cogitated upon what he knew about dreams and their symbols.

Dream symbolism has its own logic, he considered. In truth, it was more intuitive and irrational than what a rational mind could fathom or understand. The language of the unconscious was exactly that, a language. Like every known language, it had a vocabulary and a syntax. Although primarily visual, it was as full of meaning as any of the written or spoken languages that existed. Unlike spoken languages, however, where, for instance, a cigar is always a cigar, unless the word was being used as a metaphor, an object was exactly that... an object.

However, a cigar in the dream world could have a variety of different meanings (and as Freud is attributed as saying, sometimes a cigar is just a cigar, so it was all very tricky indeed). Robert decided that the key was to stay focused and alert. He would be especially mindful and pay extra special attention, to everything. If some higher intelligence was at work here, if some one or some thing was guiding him or pulling the strings of his reality, it must be for a purpose; paying attention was therefore, essential.

Ironically, as he was having this mental conversation about the necessity of being present to what was happening, he had walked mindlessly through the streets of the small town and ended up in a residential neighborhood.

"Robert? Robert?" a woman's voice shouted. Robert paid attention and immediately walked quickly in the direction that the voice had come from.

"Robert? Robert, where are you?" the woman's voice grew louder as he approached. Standing at the front door of a house, Robert recognized his own mother, except that now she looked as she had back in the sixties, younger and more vibrant.

"Mom, is that you?" Robert said, as he got closer, "I'm over here."

Completely ignoring him, she turned into the house. Robert suddenly realized that this was his childhood home; there was the swing in the front yard, crooked and rusted; the huge maple tree, the rickety fence that always needed mending, the stuff of his memories surrounding him.

"Hello?" he called, as he walked through the open front door. Getting no answer, he walked into the kitchen. The younger version of his mother was preparing supper. He stood just inside the door for what seemed like a long time, waiting for his mother to greet him. She was entirely focused upon mixing and then kneading bread. Was she purposefully ignoring him? Had he upset her in some way? Would the shock of her seeing him all grown up be too upsetting? Was her mind protecting her from a shock by not registering his presence in her brain?

"Mom," he said softly, "it's me, Robert." Again, his mother gave no indication that she had heard his voice and instead, stuck to her task. I'm invisible to her, he reasoned. I must be here simply as an observer. I must pay even closer attention. His father, Franklin, who appeared to be somewhere in his thirties, popped his head into the kitchen.

"Pop?" Robert said, automatically. Ignoring Robert, and acting like he was upset about something, Franklin addressed his wife.

"Did you find him?" he asked.

"No," Anita responded, "and supper is almost ready."

"He's going to get it, tonight," Franklin said ominously and walked straight past Robert, as if he didn't exist. I suppose, Robert thought, in their reality, I do not.

Robert walked out into the yard at the back of the house. Overwhelmed by a wave of nostalgia, he breathed in the all-too-familiar back yard, his one-time private play ground. Overgrown with unkempt trees and wild grass, it was his very own jungle where, as a child, he had many adventures. It was in this place where his imagination ran riot. From here he had traveled to distant places including Africa, the East Indies, Australia and the rainforests of the Amazon. From the trees he had followed the silk route to Asia, stopping off in Benghazi, Bengali, Timbuktu and Zaire, and any other exotic place, even if it wasn't directly on the route.

As he walked more deeply into the tree-strewn yard, he heard a rustling and a murmuring sound. Looking up, he saw his old tree house, home-made and ramshackle; a hobbled together mismatch of old wood and left-over lumber hung over the yard. Looking through the cracks, he saw a lighted candle flickering. As he got closer, he discovered that the muttering sound came from a little boy who was playing inside of the tree house.

Robert quietly walked around the rear, to where a larger gap in the wood appeared, until he could see the little boy engrossed in play. That's one of my Lost Boys, Robert realized, as he recognized one of the boys that had chased him earlier (one of the two whom he had feared were monsters or dragons). He smiled in recollection of his former ludicrous thought. As he observed his current boyhood self, he was struck by what a sensitive and shy little boy this was. The child was entirely captivated by his make-believe game .

What Robert slowly became struck by, although perhaps it should have been deeply meaningful from the start, was that what he was looking at was not some random kid or Lost Boy. It was his very own self, just as he was, when he was a tender ten year old. Tears formed in his eyes; his heart softened with a plurality of loving feelings. As his mind filled with a number of dissonant, unclear memories, the emotional richness of the moment was almost too overwhelming for Robert to contemplate or be present to for long.

"Move the tanks in first and then the infantry," ten year old Robert said as he moved little toy soldiers about. "No," he corrected, "tanks first. Like this…" Little Robert moved around some toy tanks and, adorably to big Robert, added his own sound effects as he did so.

"How's it going, Robert?" grown up Robert said to his younger self. Seemingly oblivious, little Robert continued with his toy battle.

"Robert?" Anita, his young mother called from the house.

"Yes?" answered both Roberts, simultaneously.

"Go get cleaned up for supper."

"Coming," said young Robert.

"Now, Robert! Your father's been looking all over," Anita said as she came from the house. Young Robert bounded down the tree house ladder and ran right past grown up Robert towards the house.

Robert walked back into the house and took his time. He surveyed the home and examined all of the nooks and crannies of its interior, matching the images he saw now with those of his memories. Climbing the stairs, he checked out the once-familiar baseball prints hanging on the wall. Hearing his father's voice, he followed it to his old bedroom. The door was open and Robert could see prints and posters hanging on the walls, a mix of baseball legends, super heroes and pop stars.

"Tell me again why you didn't come in to supper the first time that you were called," the younger version of his father asked young Robert.

"I told you, I was playing soldiers with Willy the Wizard," replied young Robert, defensively and expecting the worst.

"How many times do I have to tell you that there is no such person as Willy the Wizard? Why do you persist with these lies?"

"I'm not lying, father," answered young Robert, tears gathering in his eyes, his voice quivering, "playing soldiers was his idea, not mine."

Young Franklin grabbed his son by the shoulders to straighten him, bring him face to face and to further emphasize his seriousness, "I'm going to give you one more chance, young man. I do not take kindly to liars. Why didn't you come to supper when your mother called you? Have you no respect for your parents?"

"I didn't hear… I was playing soldiers…" Young Robert was sobbing now, knowing what was coming next. Watching with growing trepidation, Robert also knew what was coming. He watched the scene with a growing mix of familiarity and disgust.

Click. The sound of his father's belt buckle as metal clicked on metal and his father undid his belt. Swoosh. The sound the belt made when his father pulled it, by the buckle, out of his pants loops. Robert watched, helplessly, as Franklin, the younger version of his father, removed the leather belt from his trousers. How can a man be so cruel, he thought? The kid is only ten years old, surely this innocent offense didn't merit a beating…

"Turn around," Franklin ordered his son before Robert could finish his thought. As if he had done it many times, young Robert turned and bent forward over his father's resting leg.

"NO!" Robert shouted as Franklin raised the belt, and then, wham, swung it down as hard as he could to connect with young Robert's proffered small bottom. Again and again the belt rose and swung down. The blend of slaps made by leather against a small child's bottom, and the child's tearful crying, were almost a too potent maddening mix. Robert, outraged, felt powerless and useless in his limited capacity as an observer.

"Leave him alone, you big jerk!" Robert yelled at his young father., "Leave the kid alone!" It was as if Robert himself felt each of the slaps and every ounce of fear, anger and humiliation that his young self was too afraid or too numb and wounded to feel as he took his punishment. Robert watched the tiny person that he was take it, as his father had always told him to do, 'like a man.'

"You no good abuser..." Robert vented, unable to look at his young father without feeling a bitter mix of anger and disgust. "You emotionless, cold, son of a bitch!"

After what seemed like an interminable age, Franklin stopped swinging his weapon and allowed his son to fall onto the bed. The little boy, his face tear-stained and red, looked like a crumpled toy. Franklin stood up and replaced his leather belt.

"Go wash up for supper," Robert's father said, as he left the room.

As Robert watched his young father leave, he didn't care to justify what he considered was unjustifiable behavior. He was disinterested in the treatment Franklin himself may have experienced, at the hand of his own father when he was little, even if it was ten or twenty times worse, that led to this moment. There was no excuse for such criminal and abusive behavior; such cruel and unusual punishment meted out to an innocent and helpless young child. Robert felt the pain of the young boy who was hurt beyond the mere physical. In fact, the soreness of the flesh was the easiest pain to take. It was the psychological and emotional ache which was the hardest to experience and to recover from; the guilt, the shame, and the humiliation were deeply damaging.

Overcome with compassion for his younger self, Robert sat on the bed and placed his hand on the young boy's shoulder. Young Robert buried his face into his pillow and cried, his body still shaking from the terror and trauma of the beating.

"That's it, little guy, let it all out. I know exactly how you feel."

As if young Robert heard him, he stopped crying and turned to look up at Robert, his older self. Does he see me? thought Robert, as he felt a look of total love and understanding pass between them. Young Robert then buried his head into Robert's chest as Robert warmly embraced him. The child Robert then released the remainder of his pent up tears.

"That's it, little fella," Robert said softly, "go ahead and have yourself a good cry. Everything will work out just fine, you'll see. Everything's going to work out, just fine." Robert kissed the head of his former child self and rocked him gently in a soothing embrace. Tears formed in and fell from Robert's own eyes; it was the first time that he had cried in a very long time.

A dream is a microscope through which we look at the hidden occurrences in our soul.

~Erich Fromm

An alarm went off and Robert woke in his own bed, in the present day, sobbing and hugging his pillow. He oriented himself to his room, turned off his alarm and got up to start his day. Feeling numb and a little checked out, he drove to work with classical music on, for its calming effect. He was not aware of thinking about anything in particular as he rode the elevator to his office floor. When the doors opened, he remembered that there was a barrier again blocking his office. Looking into the reception area, the barrier was revealed.

He remained in the elevator, not knowing what to do and, in truth, not really caring what happened next. Alison and Harding were both standing at the reception desk. They watched him with puzzlement as, after a moment, the elevator doors closed. As he disappeared from their sight, Robert gave them a feeble wave. He wasn't quite sure why he did that, it was an automatic gesture.

Robert waved another weak wave to Tom, the day security guy, who waved back and made a note in the log book. As he left the front of the building, Robert realized that his car was in the parking lot, which was actually behind the building. Deciding not to go through the building again, and risk looking like a complete idiot, he turned the corner. He intended to round the block. After stepping into the side street, he stopped dead.

To his surprise, he was back in Pentonville again. Retracing his steps, back around the front of the building, he hoped that he might return to the present day. No such luck. He looked around at the people, places and cars. It all suggested another time in the past, not the 60s which he had so recently re-visited. What era are we in now, he wondered. Is this the seventies?

"There he is!" a young man's voice yelled out. Three youths ran up to Robert. He immediately recognized them as Dean, Cory and, the ringleader of the group, Travis.

"Where have you been, man?" asked Travis in a frenzy, "we've been looking all over."

"Jerome's pissed," Cory added, "we're going to lose the gig."

"Travis!" said Robert warmly, "Cory... Dean, how are you kids doing?"

"No time, man," said Travis, pulling Robert along, "move it."

Robert went along, without resistance or interest. It was as if he had decided to allow the dream events to unfold, as if he were riding a roller coaster ride. Where will this take me now, he wondered. As they turned off of the familiar main streets and into the side streets, Robert remembered the past that he was currently in. They had a weekly gig in Jerome's Bar. It was a dive bar in the working class section of the town which had live jazz bands playing most days of the week. As they entered, Travis waved to Jerome, a black man in his sixties or maybe seventies, it was hard to tell. His demeanor suggested that he had seen just about everything in his challenge-filled lifetime.

"We're all here, now, Jerome," Travis said in his best imitation adult voice. "It's all cool, man."

Jerome nodded. He didn't seem put out either way as he served his mixed yet mostly black clientele.

Robert smiled with fond remembrance of the place; the dingy furniture, the worn carpet, the musty, alcohol-infused aroma of the joint triggered memories of happy times. His reveries made him appear goofy and out of it. His demeanor was a concern to the others, who were frazzled and anxious that their gig be a success.

"I need to know, man," said Travis to Robert, in all seriousness, "are you loaded or are you cool?" Robert was looking all around, checking out the really neat lighting fixtures, still taking his personal ride down memory lane, while Travis waited for an answer.

"I remember this place," Robert said, more to himself than anyone else. His response scared the daylights out of the others. Travis grabbed him by the shoulders and looked him straight in the eye.

"Are you loaded or cool?"

"I'm cool, I'm cool," insisted Robert, holding back a wry smile at their dialogue.

"Then grab your piece and let's play," said Travis. The boys jumped up onto the small stage and grabbed their instruments. As Travis pushed a clarinet into Robert's hands, Robert looked at it with a mix of awe and nostalgia. He hadn't held a clarinet in his hands since… well, since that very day. A sudden sense of impending dread filled his being, he wasn't sure what it meant. He looked up. He could see himself in a dirty mirror hanging on the far wall. He had to do a double-take, as the reflection he was looking at didn't make sense. Looking back at him was a gawky youth of nineteen, timidly holding a clarinet in his unsure hands.

"Let's go guys!" yelled Travis with a great sense of urgency, as he now sat ready at his drum kit. "Hit it!" he said, starting the set off with a percussion intro. Dean, on bass joined in, soon followed by Cory on piano. Robert stood, frozen. Feeling the eyes of the band and the audience on him, waiting for him to 'get with it,' he realized that he could no longer continue as a detached spectator in his own dream. He needed to act, to do something, to propel the story—his story–forward. The most natural action was to put the clarinet to his lips and play. He knew the tune; it was 'Georgia On My Mind' and he used to be able to play it blindfolded. But that was a long time ago, another lifetime, as far as he was concerned. It was back in the day, when he ate, slept, dreamt, listened to and played jazz all the time.

Looking at all of the expectant faces, even if it really was a dream, Robert didn't want to let anybody down, least of all his friends who were trying so hard. Belatedly, he noticed that his left foot was already tapping out the beat. Maybe I should just put the thing to my mouth and play. If it stinks, it stinks; he figured he was going to get booed, either way, whether he played or didn't play. Maybe it's like riding a bicycle…

As Travis and the guys exchanged very worried looks, Robert finally put the clarinet to his lips, waited for the correct beat, and played. Surprising himself greatly, he didn't suck. Closing his eyes to concentrate solely on the music, he found himself back in a time when this was the moment he lived for. Something in him remembered the sheer joy of playing, the sheer exuberance of losing himself in the grace and beauty of the music. It was as if he was the music, which, as clichéd as it sounded, was the only way he could describe what he was feeling. This is living, he said to himself; in fact, this was the most alive he had felt in forever, since he could not remember when.

Why haven't I been doing this? some dormant part of him queried in the space between the notes. Heady. This is heady, said another part of himself as it happily awoke from its slumber. Robert couldn't keep track of the music, his upsurge of mixed feelings and overlapping random thoughts, occurring all at the same time, were discombobulating. Yet, that's exactly what he seemed to be experiencing lately. He had constantly experienced feelings, thoughts, memories, dreams, and reality, in an interchanging, ever shifting, mélange of mixed experience.

It's complicated, he said to himself; it's simple and yet it's complicated and it's beautiful and... I don't want it to stop. This is expression, this is living. As long as I do my part and stay with the rhythm... the ebb and flow... with the music, I'll be fine.

When he opened his eyes, he caught his reflection again in the mirror. What he saw was a nineteen year old kid, crazy in love with jazz, entirely giving himself over to the music. He remembered pure happiness. The other boys played well. Like jazz old timers, who have played with each other for decades, they played in sync. Even the most jaded of the bar patrons bobbed and nodded to the beat of the boys' music. An old timer at the bar leaned over to Jerome and whispered to him:

"So that's why you let a bunch of teenagers cut loose in your place on a Sunday afternoon. These cats can play."

Robert ended the tune with a brief clarinet solo. As soon as he removed the reed from his lips, the bar erupted in earnest and well-earned applause. The boys looked at each other, their infectious, goofy grins revealed a mix of pride, innocence, surprise and aliveness.

"Stormy Weather," Travis whispered to the boys, cueing up the next tune.

Robert's body froze. He felt as if he were made of ice. He had no idea why. His senses went on high alert, as if he were expecting something terrible to happen but did not know exactly what. Robert scanned the room for potential trouble but didn't see anyone acting unusual or notice anything untoward. He began to play, at first, with trepidation. Then, as the tune got hot, a warm, melting feeling grabbed hold of him again and he dissolved into the rhythm.

This time, he lost himself completely in the music. Eyes closed and swooning, he didn't see the shaft of light snake inward as the front door opened and daylight streamed in. Like a trespasser, the sunlight breached the inner sanctum of the dark and smoky chamber. In the dark doorway, the sunlight casting a halo around him, stood the shadow of Robert's father, Franklin. He wore a look of disgust and rage on his disapproving visage.

Squinting his eyes in search of his son, Franklin stormed through the bar. He spotted Robert and mid-song, leapt up on stage and grabbed the clarinet right out of his son's mouth. All of the music abruptly stopped; the jazz bar clientele looked confused and disoriented, as if they had just been woken from a deep sleep.

Time slowed down for Robert. His father pulled him roughly from the raised stage and moved him past his stunned band mates and the puzzled jazz lovers and the owner of the bar. Everyone exchanged inquiring looks, as if wondering if someone should stop him or interfere. No one did.

"I could have you closed down, serving alcohol to minors," Franklin said to Jerome as he sailed past. Jerome watched the scene unfold without expression, obvious emotion or sign of an increased heart beat. Robert's last image was of a chorus of faces, all turned his way, watching his plight with a mix of expressions ranging from shock to shared humiliation. The snap shot, he realized, was frozen still and seemed forever etched deep into his psyche.

His face flushed red with rage, Franklin drove Robert's former self, a shell of his former joyous self, toward home. He was forced into the back seat, as punishment. It also seemed to be a statement that he was 'not being good enough' to sit in the front, like a normal, civilized person.

"How dare you! You know better than to think that it's okay to hang out in a saloon on Sunday afternoon, with a crowd of lowlife alcoholics!" Franklin raged. "I didn't raise you to be a reprobate! Playing music like some kind of performing monkey for the amusement of a bunch of damn," he paused before he actually said the word, or maybe he couldn't think of a better slur, "...drunks," he finally said, as if throwing a verbal hand grenade.

As a final display of his disapproval, Franklin rolled down the window and hurled Robert's clarinet high into the air. Looking back, out the rear window, Robert saw the instrument float though the air in slow motion. As if held aloft by the wind, it seemed to linger in the air, for some time, twisting slowly and delicately before it came to earth. It landed with a thud on the solid tarmac and several parts broke off. It bounced several times, before it finally came to rest. It was a sad and lonely testament to Robert's perception of his relationship with his dad. Suffering the final ignominy, Robert watched with horror as an oncoming car approached and its tires crushed the discarded clarinet. That's exactly how I am feeling inside, he thought to himself. That's it exactly. I am crushed.

"I want you to get this music nonsense out of your head, and pay more attention to your studies," Franklin admonished. "You don't see it now but you'll thank me in the years to come, when you have a successful career and making good money. I know I may seem harsh, but I'm only doing what's best for you in the long run."

Robert stared at the back of his father's head, consumed with a mixture of hatred and disgust.

For often, when one is asleep, there is something in consciousness which declares that what then presents itself is but a dream.

~Aristotle

Robert awoke with a sore neck. He had fallen asleep sitting upright in a chair by his father's hospital bed. He had no idea how long he had dozed off for. The hospital wards and corridors were busy with people which suggested that it was day time or perhaps early evening. On the other side of the bed, in another chair, sat his mother. She had apparently also dozed off and was still in a deep sleep. Robert woke her with a gentle shake.

"Do you want me to take you home?" he asked.

"No, son," she said groggily, "I'm okay to drive." They left the hospital. Robert walked his mom to her car and told her to drive carefully. When he reached and got into his own car, and put the key into the ignition, he felt a pang of loneliness. He did not look forward to going home to an empty house. As he drove through the city streets, the flashing neon sign of a store caught his eye. Pulling over, he saw that it was a music store. The neon sign was musical notes on a staff. Robert quickly parked and walked into the store. The window display housed every conceivable musical instrument but only one got his interest. It was a beautiful sleek and shiny, African hardwood clarinet.

Robert felt like an excited kid watching the store clerk box it up and place it carefully into a shopping bag.

"I don't suppose you happen to know some good live jazz venues in town?" Robert inquired.

"For live jazz," the store clerk mentally ran through his live music venue list, "you don't have a lot of choices. Most of it is that smooth jazz stuff," he said derisively, "but, if you don't mind slumming it a little, Wallace's Bar on Third has the best live jazz around."

Unassuming from the outside, cozy and intimate on the inside, Wallace's Bar was not too dissimilar from Jerome's from Robert's past. As Robert entered, he heard the warm and familiar sound of a jazz trio: double bass, piano and drums. Taking a seat at the bar, Robert ordered a drink from a friendly bartender, or maybe it was the owner tending bar, the bar's namesake. Robert figured that he would chat to the guy a bit later, when the musicians took a break.

Robert tried to remember, but couldn't figure out when he had last actually been in a bar. He realized then, that he had been missing out on a truly stimulating experience. The musicians weren't legends, but how often do you get a chance to hear decent live music? And the place was so cozy, dark and intimate; it was the best type of venue to experience jazz. In fact, in his mind, listening to jazz in a dive bar was the ideal way to most deeply appreciate that particular musical form.

It was more than an auditory experience; the physical environment and atmosphere played a large part in the more complete jazz package: the dim lights, the stale scent of booze emanating from the carpet, the counter, and maybe even the furniture and the walls of the place; the clientele as well, appreciative jazz aficionados who listened with rapt attention as the music rose and fell like emotion. Nobody noticed or cared as Robert sat at the bar nursing a beer and with a sweet, childlike grin, breathing in the auditory, olfactory and kinesthetic moment.

Robert stayed till closing. He didn't get a chance to chew the fat with the cool bartender. Even as he was leaving, he told himself that he would be back; this was going to be his new hangout from now on. Gail will totally understand, he said to himself; maybe she would accompany him on date night. Though, upon reflection, he knew that it wouldn't be her kind of scene. Also, feeling compelled to make conversation, instead of listening raptly to the music, would defeat the entire purpose of his going.

Robert arrived back at his home with a spring in his step that he hadn't had when he left that morning. Indeed, he hadn't been so energized in a very long time. He felt change happening inside him, maybe something inside that had been asleep, or lying dormant, was waking. He wasn't quite sure what it was but it felt good and he liked it. Deciding to have a nightcap, he went to the alcohol cabinet. Pouring himself a drink, he remembered that he still had his old jazz vinyl collection stashed underneath. He leaned down to unearth it.

Leafing through the old records took him back in time: he had Miles Davis, Artie Shaw, Benny Goodman, Woody Herman and more. He smiled with recognition, as some of the albums triggered the memory of happier moments in his life. He chose Miles Davis' "Kind Of Blue" and took it to his old Technics turntable. The turntable hadn't been played over the years and had become more a quaint piece of art furniture than a working stereo system. Checking it out, he saw that it was covered with dust and wasn't even plugged in.

Probably wouldn't even work anymore, he mused with sadness. When he plugged the connector into the wall outlet, he smiled with hope as the light on the turntable came on. Placing the album on the turntable socket, he carefully picked up the arm and dropped it delicately on the rim of the twelve inch record. As Robert increased the volume to an acceptable level, the room filled with the majestic sound of Bill Evans on piano, Paul Chambers on bass, Jimmy Cobb on drums and of course, Miles Davis on trumpet. Robert sat back in the armchair, closed his eyes and almost swooned.

As he listened to the velvety blues of his jazz heroes, he realized that whatever had awoken in him, repressed passion, a soul-yearning for beauty, whatever it was, revealed the truth of his situation. Ever since he had repressed his passion for music, he had lived a passionless, soulless existence. In short, he felt that for some years he had not really been living at all. He had been merely existing.

What is a life lived without passion? he asked himself. And what is passion, but a yearning of the soul for recognition and self-expression? The beauty within seeks beauty without. Perhaps we require beauty as a needed reflection and acknowledgment and confirmation of its own existence. If we fail to recognize beauty, it may wither and die.

Is this what Gail has been a witness to over the years? he wondered, sadly. Has she observed the slow death and disappearance of my inner beauty, my inner passion and light? Even though she hadn't articulated it is this what she was alluding to when she said that I was living a life of habit and routine, with little really to interest me?

Robert was now horrified that in retrospect, there was nothing in his life that he seemed to look forward to beyond their weekly Friday date-night ritual of dinner and a movie. Why hadn't he seen this earlier? He was a highly-trained, practicing, very rational, dream therapist, after all. In hindsight, he could see himself so clearly. What an absolute bore I've became, he reflected.

The fire in the belly, which he could feel so definitively now, must have been absent for a long time. It wasn't just a matter of getting older and mellowing to the piss and vinegar anger of rebellious youth, not at all. It's as if some life impulse, some form of self or soul-expression had gotten extinguished and what had been left to exist was but a crust of his former self.

He didn't feel like this was self pity, or indulgent, but he could hear a crying inside. It was as if a tender part of self was lamenting all of the lost years, the many years of emotional numbness and lack of inspiration. He had abided in a cold place, alone, without the warmth of the fire of his own soul and passion. He grieved over the years and years spent in sterile emotional isolation, cut off from the world and his loved ones and more seriously still, his very own self. Who the hell am I, really? he wanted to know.

Did it all end for me that night in Jerome's Bar? Was that the moment that my inner light got extinguished? He hadn't picked up a musical instrument since that evening. Nor had he dared to listen to his heretofore prized jazz collection.

When the album played to its conclusion, and the arm of the turntable reset itself into its armrest, Robert cast his eyes over to where he had placed his purchase of the day. He stared at his shiny new clarinet. Unboxing it with reverence, his eyes scanned the shiny black lacquered wood, keywork, tone holes and single reed with fervent approval. When he ran his finger tips over the key holes, it surprised him when the skin on his arms rose with goose bumps. If he placed the beautiful woodwind to his lips, would he still remember how to play? Perhaps something of my former ability still remains, he thought.

Nervously placing the clarinet to his lips, he positioned his fingers over the key holes and blew into it. The sound which he produced sounded like the screeching of tires just prior to a traffic accident. I need a little help, he thought. Placing the needle of the turntable on a selected track of the Miles Davis album, he decided that it might be more helpful to his memory banks if he had some accompaniment.

"I'll jam with Miles," he said cheekily. Then he grinned to himself.

Tapping his right foot to the intro, Robert waited for his cue. Blowing softly, he tried to get out of his own way and let his memory do the rest. It wasn't pretty but he would only get better. Despite hitting an abundance of bum notes, Robert got more and more into it as the clarinet warmed up. He could feel his heart soar as he jammed with Miles and the boys. His fingers weren't as limber and responsive as they used to be. He tried not to let his frustrations ruin the moment.

Tears welled in his eyes as he took his clarinet solo. His playing was so out of tune, it was laughable. Right now, though, all he wanted to do was play. A grand mix of emotions swirled about his consciousness, threatening to sabotage his playing. If he gave the emotions an inch of his attention, they would surely take a yard and flood his body and mind with upset and negative emotions that would create mental torment.

Cognizant that emotional Barbarians were bearing down on him made him play harder. His efforts created more and more errors. His fingers lost the plot and as if separated from his mind and the music, they marched to a different drumbeat all on their own. The sounds which he created were now so far divorced from the music on the LP that that he knew he had to stop and be present to the emotional tornado raging inside of him.

As soon as he made his fingers stop playing, the forces of anger and rage within him weakened his body. He buckled at the knees and his body dropped to the floor. He was flooded with a torrent of mental and emotional pain. His breathing became labored and his body shook, as if he were going into shock. The force and scale of his own deep anguish frightened him. He couldn't remember having any such episode in the past and wasn't fully sure what was happening now. Is this a panic attack? he asked himself. His therapist self had kicked in. This part of him knew about this from his studies and from books, though he hadn't treated anyone with the affliction.

His heart pounded in his chest. He knew that his own fear of what was happening to him was making matters worse. Although aware that his terror was facilitating a vicious circle, he felt mentally and emotionally incapable of stopping the cycle. Feeling out of control and incapable of stopping it made him feel more afraid. Then he heard a cheeky part of him say, inside of his own mind, that's what a vicious circle is, you dummy. He could for the first time equate the feeling of severe panic with the symptomatic description listed in the Diagnostic and Statistical Manual of Mental Disorders that had served as his occupational bible since he left college.

As he crawled to the nearest armchair, Robert unplugged the turntable at the wall outlet and the music came to an abrupt and irreverential stop. Searching in his mind for the source of his anguish, he knew that he wouldn't have to dig too far. In fact, curiously, his emotions, memories and feelings were all pretty close to the surface now.

His father, his father, his father… like a monotonous mantra, repeating inside his mind, he was aware that he could no longer repress the pent up rage which he felt towards his father. He had never been aware of it, much less expressed it. It's killing me, he thought to himself. I have to let it out or it will poison me to death. Talk to my father, he remembered the instruction he had heard not so long ago. Sure, I'll talk to my father, he countered with fury. I'll talk to that old man, all right!

Energized by the surge of anger and rage, he jumped up from his chair and left the house. It may be after midnight, and well past visiting hours, but what of it? The man's in a coma and if I wake him up from his torpor, I'd only be doing him a favor. Besides, Robert told himself, he deserves a talking to. He's only had it coming since I was a kid. He's unconscious, I can say what I want; it's not like I'll be hurting the man's feelings.

> *Dreams are true while they last, and do we not live in dreams?*

> ~Alfred Lord Tennyson

A man on a mission, Robert entered the hospital feeling less angry than he had when he had left his house. Yet he knew that he still had enough juice left to give the old man a piece of his mind. Stepping off of the elevator on the correct floor, he looked down the hall to see if the coast was clear. Waiting until a nurse turned a corner, he quietly quickened his pace. Then, unseen, he entered the room where his father lay. Still hooked up to life support machines, his father's state remained unchanged. Robert stood close to his father and without having first prepared a speech in his head, he started talking to him.

"I've so much to say to you but… I'm afraid of what's going to come out. It's the hatred I feel for you that scares me the most. You ruined my life." Robert sat down for a moment, and waited to speak, to let what he had just said sink in.

"I know I disappointed you, dad," Robert continued, in a more reasoned tone, "I never did become a successful medical doctor, like you wanted, or rather I did, but as we both know, you don't consider a doctor of the mind to be any kind of doctor, at all, do you? I'm not a professional musician, either. I guess you're especially happy about that. Looks like neither of us got what we wanted."

Considering his father's medical condition, Robert tried, but failed, to find some compassion in his heart for this man.

"And now you want one of my kidneys? I don't think so. Why not just take the plunge? Are you finally too afraid of something?" Feeling a tingling sensation, and a sudden greater sense of calm and peace, Robert looked across and saw the Elusive Lady sitting in the chair opposite. She watched him with a look of total love and acceptance.

"What do you want?" Robert asked her, quizzically. Her demeanor didn't change. "You don't even exist," he continued. "You're just in my head, right? You represent my conscience? You're my superego?"

The Elusive Lady smiled, as if he had just told a joke. Her beautiful smile broke his negative mood, he smiled too.

"So, are you going to answer me back or will I just continue to look silly?" he asked with a self-conscious smile.

The night nurse opened the door, not expecting to see Robert in the chair.

"Oh. What are you doing here?" she inquired, "it's two AM! You need to leave, right away."

Robert playfully cocked his thumb and pointed his index finger, creating a gun from his hand, and mock shot the Elusive Lady, as if to say, 'see you later.' Looking in the direction that Robert seemed to be pointing, the nurse's heart suddenly melted.

"You know what?" she said softly to Robert, "stay awhile. If you're visiting him this late, you must love him very much, right?"

"Yes. Thank you," said Robert. Then she checked on his father, made some notes in his charts, closed the door and left. When he turned back, the Elusive Lady was gone. Robert continued to sit with his father, but all of his rage and anger had dissipated. He took stock of his surroundings and tried to put everything that was going on into some kind of context. Where was he? What had happened to his life? Unable to answer or piece it all together and make sense of things, he felt alone and very small, almost like a child. He wished he could have his normal life back but when he reflected more deeply about that, the epiphany that he'd had earlier echoed again in his mind. He had not been living a life in the first place.

The next morning, Robert showed up at work tired. His clothes were wrinkled and his appearance decidedly unkempt. He had obviously failed to shower and shave. As the elevator doors opened, he immediately saw that the barrier was still present. Unable to face another pointless and extremely distressing confrontation, he found himself pressing the button to return to the ground floor. Alison had been standing just outside the elevator and, as the doors began to close, had obviously pressed the button on the outside.

"Are you leaving again, Doctor Monro?" she asked, her voice full of concern.

"Yes, cancel my appointments, will you?"

"Will you be back on Monday?" Her eyes were wide with worry.

"Yes. Back Monday. I… uh, my father, I was at the hospital all night," Robert said, then he pressed the ground floor button again and was terribly thankful when the doors closed and he didn't have to see the apprehension on Alison's face.

Robert didn't plan on leaving the city but that's what he found himself doing. He didn't take the usual route home to his empty house. Then the idea that a drive in the country side would help clear his head and maybe aid him in getting his thinking to become clearer, flitted through his mind. Once outside the concrete jungle, he found that he naturally relaxed a bit.

He drove aimlessly though scenic roads and small towns that he would normally have found quaint and charming. Instead, he was beginning to feel as aimless and uprooted as his unplanned, impulsive, directionless drive. Like a boat without an anchor, he felt himself drifting on an unforgiving ocean. His life direction, his purpose and, very possibly, his very existence felt out of his control and at the mercy of unknown elements.

As he drove back into the city, the rain clouds opened their watery load and to compound it all, Robert groaned loudly when he hit serious rush hour traffic. He developed a headache, as he struggled through the stop and go traffic. He yearned for his wife and son. He missed them so much. Their continuing absence was a wound in his heart. Dreading going back to a cold and empty house, he longed for the comfort and sanctuary of a safe, warm and familiar place where he would feel happy. The only place that came to mind was Wallace's Bar.

"How are you doing there, partner?" the bartender greeted Robert as he entered and sat at the bar.

"I'll have to get back to you on that," answered Robert and conjured up his best social laugh, "the jury's still out." The bartender nodded. He totally got it, life could be challenging.

"What can I get you?"

"I'd like a brandy." Looking around, Robert noticed that there were more people present than before and probably because it was a Friday night, it was a different mix of clientele; overall, a younger, trendier crowd sat laughing, chatting, knocking back drinks and relaxing. In fact, entirely out of Robert's sight line, Alison and her young friends were happily ensconced in a booth down the far end of the bar.

When Wallace returned with his drink, Robert asked him if there was going to be any live music any time soon. Wallace told him that a jazz quartet was scheduled, "they're pretty good, but they're not the most punctual crew so don't ask me what time they'll show up." Robert wondered to himself why the bar would tolerate such disrespect. As if Wallace were privy to his thoughts, the barkeep spoke again.

"I don't charge a cover, so I can't pay anyone to play here nightly. I give the group free drinks and whatever they make on tips. For some of them, it's good exposure; they maybe get invited to play at a wedding or something. These guys who are playing tonight all have regular jobs. They come out and play jazz together for the love of it. You here for the jazz?"

"Yes," answered Robert, "I just discovered your bar. A referral."

"Enjoy," said Wallace, as he was called away by another customer.

Robert really did want to enjoy himself but when the quartet eventually showed up and as the evening wore on, Robert found himself unsuccessfully fighting off emotions of despair and pessimism. Having more brandies than his system could easily handle contributed. By the time the jazz group took their second break of the evening, Robert felt downright miserable.

"Dr. Monro?" inquired Alison as she discovered him at the bar, "what are you doing here?" She looked at him with surprise.

"What are *you* doing here?" Robert replied, more as a comment on her question.

"I'm sorry," responded Alison, realizing that her question may have seemed a bit rude, "I guess I did not expect to see you here. Are you with someone?"

"I'm not actually here," said Robert, "and neither are you."

"I don't understand," said Alison, looking to see what exactly he had been drinking.

"This is all a dream and you and everyone here are my dream characters."

"I'm a dream character?"

"Correct. You and everyone here represent something unhealed in my unconscious."

Alison quickly glanced back to check on her friends, who were oblivious to her absence. Then, partly out of curiosity, partly concern for Robert's well being, she sat down on the adjacent vacant bar stool to give him her full attention.

"That's a very interesting idea," she said, "I've tried to read your books but they're--"

"Forget my books," interrupted Robert, "they're garbage. I'm in the process of completely revising my understanding of dreams and their symbolism."

"That's fantastic. You have a new theory?"

"No, it's not a theory. It's an understanding… more of a revelatory experience. It's hard to explain because, unlike my books, it's not a mental construct. I haven't fully understood it myself yet or I would have woken up already."

"Oh, I get it," Alison said excitedly, "it's just what Miss Blessing is saying in her book, Life Is But A Dream?"

"No," rebuffed Robert, "I can't speak to that, I haven't read her book."

"But you said… we're all in a dream from which we have yet to wake from, right?"

"I'm not saying that this is a shared experience, no. I can only speak for myself. All I can say is that this is my dream, particular to my life and my unhealed issues."

"Oh," said Alison, confused.

"Look at it like this," Robert began, "The unconscious acts as a storehouse to everything that my conscious mind would rather not face or own up to or has been unable to be present to: this includes past traumas, unprocessed hurts, negative thoughts and feelings about myself and others and so on. In order to be a complete and entirely healthy, individuated person, we must reclaim all of these aspects and heal or transform these repressed issues by excavating them."

"Yes, I understand all that," said Alison.

"Yet, because maybe it's too painful for the conscious mind to face up to these issues, the unconscious alerts us to their existence by presenting them in more acceptable and less threatening disguises: they are the symbols and metaphors of our dreams, whether those dreams occur when we are awake or sleeping. If one can figure out what the dream story is all about, then you have made conscious what was unhealed in the unconscious. It's ingenious."

"So…" Alison said, tentatively, "what's the new part?"

"Up to this point I've been analyzing dreams as separate and distinct from my reality. At night we have a dream and then, when we wake up, we attempt to interpret the dream. I'm not yet sure how or why it happened but I've come to realize that I'm now interpreting the dream within the dream itself, there is no separation. Whether sleeping or waking, I'm always dreaming."

"Wow," said Alison, "that is new. That's fantastic!"

"I'm not so sure," cautioned Robert, "the problem now is that I can't seem to wake up… it's as if the dream won't let me wake up until the interpretation is complete."

"You have to solve the puzzle, before you collect the prize?"

"It's more than that," Robert considered, "I don't just have to solve it, I also have to integrate my experience. It goes beyond the mere mental and logical. It also means accessing and processing powerful and painful emotions, repressed feelings and thoughts which I'd rather not deal with… or should I say, would rather deal with them in my own time and not have them foisted upon me when it's most inconvenient."

"So, you can get trapped in a dream?" Alison asked, not entirely certain that she was understanding him correctly.

"Exactly," said Robert, "that is precisely what I am saying."

"Suppose you never get to solve it?"

"I'm not sure," answered Robert, "probably if you stay in the dream long enough, you finally get to solve it, no matter how long it takes."

"What if it took forever?"

"Time doesn't exist in the dream world, at least not as we understand it. Ever had a dream that felt like an eternity but you'd only actually been asleep for a few minutes?"

"Are you saying that you're dreaming right now?"

"That's right. We're probably both at home sleeping, right now. Maybe we're having this conversation because my dream character, who I think of as me, is trying to figure it out and my unconscious has conjured you up to play some role in helping me…" Before he could finish his statement, Alison's friends joined them. They wished to leave the bar. As one of them handed her her coat they pulled her along to take her with them.

"I have to go now, Dr. Monro, but it was very nice talking to you," said Alison as she was dragged away. Robert gave her a friendly wave and noticed that the musicians were again set up to play. They were just a few beats into their new set when Robert's body froze: the group was playing 'Stormy Weather.'

Robert again experienced the familiar symptoms of an intense anxiety attack: he felt a panicked sense of foreboding, pounding heart, nausea, dizziness and an urgent, almost desperate, desire to flee. He fought it as long as he could but it only got stronger.

Outside the bar, Alison and her friends waited for another friend to bring the car around. As the car pulled up, Alison turned and saw Robert staggering from the bar. Telling her friends to go on without her, she went to Robert's aid.

"Dr. Monro, are you okay?" A look of terror on his face, he hugged the wall, and then slid to the ground. "Should I call an ambulance?" she asked urgently. Robert shook his head, no, then burst into tears, and buried his face in his hands.

"It's okay, Dr. Monro," soothed Alison, placing her arm around him, "let it all out."

Dreams say what they mean, but they don't say it in daytime language.

~Gail Godwin

Robert awoke in semi-darkness in a strange bed in an unfamiliar room. He could see that a giant teddy bear rested beside him in the bed. Hanging from the ceiling were flying angels; the ceiling had a Botticelli-like mural painted upon it. Murals on the room walls depicted scenes of surreal beauty; the room itself was cluttered with toy fairies, unicorns and other mythological creatures. Getting out of the bed, he noticed that he was fully dressed. He left the bedroom and quietly walked to the living room. It was filled with artworks and sculptures, many of them works in progress. Alison stood before a large canvas, painting passionately. Unseen, Robert watched, marveling at her skill and artistry.

"That's absolutely beautiful," he said softly. Alison jumped in shock, the paintbrush flying from her hand. "I'm sorry, I didn't mean to…"

"What are you doing awake?" Alison queried, retrieving her brush, "it's 4 A.M."

"I just woke up, I guess," answered Robert, uncertainly.

"Want some coffee?" Alison asked, now more cheerful.

"Love some," said Robert, smiling.

Robert excused himself to go to the bathroom while Alison went to the kitchen to make the coffee. When Robert rejoined her, the coffee was ready.

"You took me to your home," Robert said, stating the obvious.

"It was that or a homeless shelter. You were in pretty bad shape."

"I was doing fine, till they start playing my song."

"I know this is none of my business but are you getting professional help?" When Robert hesitated, Alison knew her answer. "It's none of my business," she said, "are you okay to drive home?"

"Yeah, sure. Did you drive my car here?"

"No," answered Alison, "we took a cab."

"I should reimburse you."

"Don't worry about it," Alison said, taking a business card magnet off the fridge, "this cab service is pretty good."

"Great," said Robert, feeling not so great. Alison returned to her work in the living room while Robert took out his cell phone to make the call. He dialed a few numbers, then stopped. Taking his coffee into the living room, he sheepishly approached Alison.

"Actually, no, I'm not getting any professional help," he said.

"Don't take this the wrong way but maybe it would be a good idea if you did."

"I know. You're right."

"Did you get through to the cab company?"

"I didn't call," Robert said, nervously, "this might sound pretty weird but I… I could really use some company, right now."

"You want to crash here?" she stared at him, her expression quizzical.

"I can't face going home to an empty house." Unused to showing his vulnerable side, and realizing how wimpy he may be sounding, Robert quickly retracted, "I'm sorry. It's not your problem. You've been really great and I appreciate your kindness. I should go."

"Finish your coffee," Alison said, firmly, "have a seat." Clearing away some artwork, she revealed a small, armchair that looked especially cozy. Robert sank into it. Looking down, he saw a box filled with copies of Miss Blessing's book.

"You're selling Miss Blessing's book?"

"I've been giving them to friends."

"The book's that good?" inquired Robert, picking one up to get a closer look.

"Miss Blessing is my mother, Dr. Monro," said Alison, noticing Robert's surprise, "I was the one that told her about you. She thinks you're brilliant, by the way."

Remembering how he had spoken of Miss Blessing, most of the time in a disparaging way, made Robert feel very uncomfortable.

"All those things I said about Miss Blessing... Why didn't you tell me that she was your mother?"

"I just did," said Alison, matter-of-factly.

"She never mentioned any kids. Why does she still go by Miss Blessing?"

"I guess because she never married."

"Oh," said Robert, wondering if he was getting into some sensitive areas, "and your father?"

"Never met him."

"I'm sorry. That must have been rough."

Unable to concentrate, Alison stopped painting.

"I should go," Robert said, standing.

"I want you to stay," replied Alison, emphatically, "I've got two tickets for the Cirque du Soleil tomorrow and curiously my friend canceled."

"Really?" said Robert, as an uncontainable smile broke wide across his face.

As Alison put away her things, Robert retired to the bedroom to get some more rest. Later that morning, he awoke to find himself hugging the cuddly, soft giant teddy. It felt great. Hearing some beautiful classical music, he assumed that Alison had gotten up before him. The music got louder as he approached the living room. Robert stood in the doorway and stared, amazed and fascinated, as Alison played a cello like a concert professional. It sounded like a Bach cello suite. The music really touched his heart. Waiting for the music to conclude, and making sure that he would be seen before he spoke, he walked into her sight line.

"Good morning," she greeted him.

"You paint beautiful paintings. You play the cello like a goddess. What are you doing working reception for a bunch of therapists?"

"One thing I've learned from my mother is that it doesn't matter what you do. It's how you do it that counts." Alison walked to the kitchen and Robert followed.

"You could play professionally. You're very gifted. Seriously."

"It's been a dream of mine since I was little," said Alison as she placed a bunch of brown twigs, tree bark and green plant stems into a large pot of boiling water.

"So, why don't you?"

"Playing in public gives me stress. Stress is not good for my condition."

"What condition?" asked Robert, his nose crinkling at the pungent smell of the boiling herbs.

"Chinese herbs," Alison explained, "helps with the pain."

"You're in pain?"

"I have lupus."

"Lupus? A disease of the immune system?"

"They don't know what it is," said Alison, wearily.

"That would explain all your sick days," said Robert, as if thinking out loud. "There's no cure for that, is there?"

Alison didn't answer, perhaps deciding that that's as far as she wanted to go with the conversation. Lost for words, anyway, Robert decided not to push it.

In the afternoon, on their way to the Cirque du Soleil show, Alison drove Robert back to his house so he could change into clean clothes. A windy, wet and cold day, sheets of silver gray rain lashed down. Showing her into the living room, he ran up the stairs so he could quickly change. Seeing some spilled vinyl records upon the floor, she bent down to look through them. As she did, a smile came to her face; she knew these artists and loved their music. Picking out a Nina

Simone album, she walked to the turntable, plugged it in and put the record on.

'I Put a Spell on You' began to play. Alison sang along sweetly. Closing her eyes, she semi-waltzed around and behind the sofa. She was oblivious to the fact that she had danced very close to a gap in the floor where the floorboard, once again, had been pulled up. She swayed to the music and took another step and screamed as she fell right through and vanished from sight.

Hearing her scream, Robert rushed down the stairs. He was now dressed in a nice blue wool sweater and jeans.

"Alison?" he called out, and looked around the living room. Robert stared in distress at Alison's purse as it rested beside the open floorboard space that led to the dream world. Oh, shit, Robert thought, fearing the worst. Oh, shit, oh, shit, oh, shit. Looking through the space, all he could see was darkness.

"Alison?" he called, not expecting a response. Terrified, he paced the room.

What to do, what to do, what to do. He thought about how kind she had been to him, putting him to bed, keeping him around when he hadn't wanted to be alone, being loving and supportive. Alison had been there for him, when he had needed her. She must be frightened in that strange and terrifying place, all alone. Summoning all his courage, he closed his eyes, held his nose and jumped into the hole.

Pause now to ask yourself the following question: "Am I dreaming or awake, right now?" Be serious, really try to answer the question to the best of your ability and be ready to justify your answer.

~Stephen LaBerge

The shock of finding himself underwater, swimming for his life, wasn't as distressing as the first time but was still terrifying, nevertheless. When his head finally bobbed above water, he sucked in air, looked around and saw that it was an amazingly sunny day. Swimming to the edge of the lake, he looked around for Alison.

"Dr. Monro!" he heard Alison call out. Looking to his right, he could make out Alison waving from a gazebo at the end of a walkway that had been built over the lake. "Isn't this fantastic?" she said, beaming.

"To be honest, I didn't have such a great time the last time I was here," Robert said, as soaking wet, he scrambled out of the water and joined her.

"What's that?" she said, pointing at something moving on a path heading in their direction. It appeared to be an elaborate, unmanned horse-drawn carriage. Alison immediately bolted towards it. "Let's investigate," she called over her shoulder, full of enthusiasm and excitement. Feeling very doubtful about the whole thing, Robert looked around for any other sign of movement or potential danger.

"Isn't it gorgeous?" Alison exclaimed, admiring the elaborately decorated carriage. The beautiful horse and colorful ornate carriage had stopped. "I think it wants us to get in," Alison said, stepping in and sitting down. She looked down at Robert, her smile wide.

"Don't you think we should be looking for a way to get out of here?" Robert said, still feeling upset by the entire experience.

"What are you talking about? This is fantastic," Alison said as she inspected the upholstery and delicate artwork which adorned the inside of the carriage.

Robert tried to remember how he had gotten out of this place the last time he was here but all he could remember was waking up in a cold sweat on his sofa in the living room.

"Come on, scaredy cat, get in," cajoled Alison, "it won't move until you get in."

It won't move? thought Robert to himself. He didn't want it to move; he wanted to get back and go to the circus, as planned. Shrugging off his fear, he took her proffered hand, and stepped up onto the running board. As soon as he did so, the horses took off.

Alison beamed with delight as the carriage transported them through some of the most picturesque pastoral landscapes she had even seen. Having leapt into the carriage, Robert, on the other hand, was preoccupied with looking out for potential threats. Looking into the distance, he saw a forest; that's where the beasts live, he noted to himself.

"I've only dreamt of places like this," Alison exclaimed joyfully.

Tranquility precedes every storm, Robert thought to himself. He did not want to share his thoughts, for fear of raining on her parade. Now what? Robert asked himself silently, as the carriage came to a stop. They had arrived at the base of a flight of steps which led up an embankment. Alison was out of the carriage and climbing the steps before Robert could suggest a discussion of strategy. "I don't know about this," he said, then followed her up the steps.

Upon reaching the top of the embankment, they both stood and looked down and saw a natural amphitheater. It was filled with people of all types and descriptions.

"Looks like a concert is about to begin," conjectured Alison, "or maybe some kind of theatrical performance or stage play, maybe."

"Or a public execution," added Robert, only half joking.

The four Munchkins from Robert's house came running up to them.

"I knew it," declared Robert, alarmed, "it's connected with the Munchkins!" Before Alison or Robert could prevent them, or react, the Munchkins hurried them along.

"We don't have much time," said Ringo, as he and his friends hurriedly hustled Alison and Robert down the steps toward the arena, "we need to hurry."

"Hurry for what? What's going on?" asked Robert as he was pushed along.

"We're two people short," answered Ringo.

"Two people short for what?" Robert countered.

Music suddenly blared from the stage as acrobats, trapeze artists, jugglers and other performers appeared on and around the theater.

"Look!" exclaimed Alison, "it's just like Cirque du Soleil!"

Robert and Alison were ushered backstage into a room that was filled with musical instruments; most were familiar but many... not so much.

"Wow," said Alison, admiringly.

"Take any instrument you want," Ringo advised.

"Really?" asked Alison, gleefully.

"Anything we want? What's the catch?" doubted Robert.

"You like?" asked Ringo as he extended a golden clarinet to Robert.

"Is this made of gold?" Robert asked, as he felt the weight and looked at it more closely.

"Beautiful timbre, don't you agree?" Ringo asked Alison as she ran a bow across a beautiful cello.

"It's amazing," marveled Alison, running the bow back and forth, again and again.

"Take them with you," Ringo said as he opened another door.

"Take them home with us?" Robert asked hopefully. As Ringo led them through a series of backstage corridors, a realization dawned on Robert's skeptical brain. "Wait a minute," Robert paused, "I hope you're not expecting us to..." Before he could finish his thought, Ringo opened an entry before them. Then the four Munchkins pushed Alison and Robert out the door. Alison and Robert stood at the back of the stage looking out at the packed and expectant theater. "Perform..." Robert said, finishing his thought.

The audience applauded them vigorously, as if they considered them the next act to perform. Already on stage, several other musicians waited for them to join them. For the first time in her visit, Alison didn't look so happy; in fact, she looked downright petrified.

"I'm too nervous to play in public," she said shakily to Robert.

"I haven't played in almost twenty years," countered Robert, equally terrified. Turning the handle to the door they just came through, Robert realized that the door was locked from the inside. "If we don't play, they'll probably kill us," Robert said, turning back to Alison. She gave him a, 'you can't be serious' look. Robert added, "No one knows we're down here."

At this point, the audience had become quiet and expectant.

"They all look so hopeful," remarked Alison, "I'd hate to disappoint them."

"I'd hate to see them pissed off," Robert added.

The musicians started to play. It was a jazz tune. Recognizing it, Robert spoke:

"That's 'Morpheus,' a John Lewis tune recorded by Miles Davis and Sonny Rollins."

"Can you play it?" asked Alison, hopefully.

"I used to be able to play it blindfolded," Robert answered.

"I'd accept a performance without a blindfold," said Alison with a smile.

The musicians gave him his cue but he missed it, so they repeated the refrain. Robert closed his eyes, tapped his foot to the beat, put the reed to his lips and played on the next cue. He played tentatively at first but, as the music heated up, he finally let it rip. Hitting one bum note after another, he admonished himself for his shit playing and stopped. As he did so, he received a genuine round of applause from the audience.

Entirely perplexed by their twisted appreciation of his awful musicianship, he took a respectful mini bow. He wondered at this turn of events. If they thought his playing was good, either they were tone deaf and didn't know the difference or they did know but didn't care. In either scenario, what was to fear, he wondered? Why not just play badly and to heck with it?

As the band started, 'It's Only A Paper Moon,' Robert played right on cue. If he was playing solo, he thought to himself, his bad playing and bum notes would be unbearable but playing with a really talented group like this, his mistakes were shielded and less noticeable. The audience became increasingly more enthusiastic and appreciative as the band covered well-known hits like, 'Tenderly,' 'Isn't This a Lovely Day,' 'Stardust,' 'Night And Day,' and so on, which buoyed Robert's confidence. Despite his bad play, he was being treated like a jazz star.

Alison had watched and listened attentively and responded enthusiastically. Although not a jazz player herself, she listened to the genre and knew most of the standards, which is what they were playing. Not having to play herself, her performance anxiety had plummeted to zero. When the band started the intro to 'Autumn Leaves,' Robert sidled up to her.

"We need a cello." Seeing Alison's body immediately tense up, Robert smiled, "hey, if I can play badly, you can play badly. Nobody here seems to care."

"I don't play jazz," Alison said nervously.

"It's not jazz," cajoled Robert, "it's 'Autumn Leaves.' Everybody knows 'Autumn Leaves,' right? Come on, play it with me."

As Robert began playing the melody, Alison stoked up her courage and very tentatively, at first, joined along. The audience responded and greeted her with a welcoming round of applause. It helped to boost her courage. Side by side, they both played the melody. As Alison became more confident and less afraid, Robert let her play the melody solo, which she nailed perfectly. The cello was so appropriate to the tune and she played it with such warmth and feeling, the audience were in a swoon.

Totally into it now, and finally truly enjoying herself, Alison played along as they covered, 'They Can't Take This Away from Me,' 'Body and Soul,' 'Someone to Watch over Me,' and 'Over The Rainbow.' When the band broke into the intro to the next song, Robert froze.

"What's wrong?" Alison asked with concern.

"It's… that song," he said, his body shaking.

Having repeated the intro to 'Stormy Weather' more than a couple times, the band stopped playing. All eyes were now focused on Robert.

"I can't," he said, answering a question no one had asked.

"Sure you can," Alison said, supportively, "it's just a song. Play with me," she said as she stroked the bow across the strings of her cello, "I'm right here with you. I know you can do it."

Hushed and attentive, it felt like the entire audience was there for him, as well. Alison's sound was soft and beautiful. The sound of the cello seemed to fill the theater and audience with a soft beautiful musical mist. Robert inhaled deeply, consciously trying to settle his nerves. A large part of him wanted to flee. If he could only run away, get somewhere safe, somewhere different, somewhere not here.

But his psychoanalyst self did not wish to succumb to fearful urges which stemmed from unhealed emotional wounds. It knew that there was no place for him to escape from his own experience; anyway, if he ran, he'd always be running. He knew that if he could get through this one song, this one time, he would be free of the urge to run, forever free. If not now, then when, he asked himself?

Tapping his foot to the beat, he placed the clarinet to his lips, waited for the correct timing and played. The sound was soft, nervous at first. He mentally gritted his teeth and allowed every demon within to depart, from their resting places, within his body, mind, soul and emotions, and fly free and soar into the light. As he did so, he felt uplifted by the grace and majesty of the heavens.

Sounding beautiful together, the cello and clarinet were then joined by the rest of the band. It was a pleasure for all concerned. He played from his core and as the tune progressed, Robert's sound became lighter, his musicianship more masterful, until finally, reaching the last note of the tune, he removed the reed from his lips and smiled the freest, most uninhibited, smile he had ever smiled in his life.

Everything looked brighter, more colorful and especially vibrant, to him now. He shared in taking a bow with his musical peers. Within the space of a few minutes, he looked like a new man, younger, lighter, happier and less troubled. He exuded joy.

The audience gave them the biggest ovation of the evening and then all the musicians joined together in the center of the stage for a curtain call, which lasted for several beautiful long minutes. The appreciation filled both Robert and Alison with bliss.

As the sun set in a glorious sky, Robert and Alison, on an adrenaline high, were ushered by the Munchkins into the horse drawn carriage.

"Thank you so much, you guys really helped us out," said Ringo, as he waved them goodbye, "you were both amazing! I'll remember this always."

"You performed in public!" Robert enthused to Alison, as the carriage took off.

"You played 'Stormy Weather', can you believe it?!" smiled Alison, sharing in his high-octane mood of excitement. "And you thought they were going to eat us!" she punched him playfully, giggling at the thought. He laughed in response.

"Well, what would you expect from creatures that live beneath the baseboards?" he responded, defending himself from her playful punching and tickling.

"We should play here again," she said, her voice warm and rich.

"What makes you think we're not stuck here forever?"

"When exactly did you become a glass half empty type of person, Dr. Monro?" Alison joked and then laughed at him a little bit.

"Enough of this Dr. Monro business," he said, evading the question, "call me Robert."

"Okay," she said, putting on a funny voice, "when did you become a dark curmudgeonly pessimist, Robert? Bob. Bobbie Boy…" Alison stopped her joking when she noticed that Robert had grown serious. "What? Did I offend you?"

"No," Robert responded in a more somber tone, "nobody's called me Bobbie Boy since college." Robert was immediately assaulted by memories of college graduation. He and Gail had graduated together. After the ceremony they had gone off together. Wearing their graduation gowns, walking on the periphery of the campus, away from the ceremony and the throng of the other graduates, Robert playfully filched Gail's cap from her head.

"Give that back, you goof," she said and smiled. Then she made an unsuccessful attempt to recover her cap.

"I told you," Robert said, placing it behind his back, "it makes you look silly."

"Does not," she said and pushed him so hard that he lost his balance and found himself falling down a slight grassy incline towards the pond. She followed and they rolled down the hill, like two excited, exiled penguins. They laughed and laughed as they tumbled and rolled over each other and the earth. They finally came to a stop, intertwined in each other's embrace. A beautiful young woman, deeply in love, Gail looked into his eyes.

"I love you, Robert. My Bobbie Boy," she said dreamily.

"I love you too, Rapunzel," he said, replacing her cap on her head and kissing her deeply with tender love.

His reverie over, Robert looked around at the beautiful landscape caught in the declining rays of a vanishing sunlight. The movement of the carriage was hypnotic and soothing. A tear ran down Robert's cheek as he observed the last remaining beams of sunlight disappear from the sky. Alison had fallen asleep, her head rested against his shoulder. The carriage ride was smooth and relaxing. Robert realized that he too was feeling very sleepy.

What a day, what a life, he thought to himself, too tired to formulate any clear thoughts or do an analysis. His eyelids felt as if they couldn't stay open a moment longer and, without any resistance from Robert's unusually peaceful mind, his eyes slowly closed.

> *Those who have compared our life to a dream were right.... We sleeping wake, and waking sleep.*
>
> ~Michel de Montaigne

Robert and Alison awoke on the sofa in Robert's house in exactly the same positions that they had been in when they had fallen asleep in the carriage. Coming fully awake, they suddenly became awkward with each other. Straightening their clothing and sitting up, they acted as if they had awoken from a beautiful dream into a cold, harsh reality. After groping for her purse, Alison was the first to stand.

"You're leaving?" Robert asked, unexpectedly disappointed.

"I'm going home to paint," she answered, retreating into her own world, "I feel so inspired!" Shyly kissing him on the cheek, she said, "see you at work, Monday?"

"Yes," Robert answered, still groggy from his slumber, "drive safely."

Robert went upstairs and got into bed. He slept an inordinate amount. Finally it was Monday morning and time to go to work. Deeply rested from all of the catch-up sleep, and transformed by his experience in the under-the-floorboard world, he felt a lightness that he wasn't quite used to yet; he liked it and secretly wondered if it was temporary or something that would last. On his drive to work he tuned his radio to a local jazz station and hummed to the tunes he knew.

He was not aware of it but, for the first time in all his commutes to work, he was the most courteous driver on the road. Stopping at the familiar intersection, the four-way stop that traditionally always got his blood boiling, he waved warmly to other drivers, gesturing when they had the right of way. Drivers that knew him, regulars on the morning commute, inexplicably found themselves waving back—before they could consciously consider what was going on and question his behavior or their own actions.

Riding the elevator up to his office, Robert wondered if the barrier would still be there. As the doors slid open, he was unperturbed to see that the barrier was, indeed, still in play. Robert's oddly peaceful frame of mind was in stark contrast to Dr. Harding's mood. Harding was unhappily fussing about the reception desk, looking for something that he did not seem able to find. "What's going on, Harding?" Robert greeted cheerily.

"Gracing us today, Monro?" Harding responded sourly, "to what do we owe the pleasure?"

"Where's Alison?"

"Alison called in sick. Again," said Harding pointedly and with obvious displeasure. "A person who calls in sick so much, obviously does not want to work."

"You don't know that," Robert said, realizing that Alison was on the verge of losing her position.

"I gave her enough warnings."

"You're firing her?"

"What's your problem?" Harding asked, stopping what he was doing. "I thought you two didn't get along?"

"I'll work her desk."

"You'll what?"

"If you promise not to fire her, I'll do her job till she gets back."

Harding took a good hard look at Robert, half wondering if something was going on that he was not aware of. "You're going to answer phones and make the coffee? Why?"

Robert settled himself behind the reception desk, tidying up the desk space. "She's a sweet kid. It's the least I can do."

"Aren't you full of surprises, lately?" Harding said, giving up on trying to decode the mystery. As he walked to his office, he turned, "I like my coffee black and with two sugars," he said and then, as an afterthought, "and get my wife on the phone, the number should be up there, somewhere." Sniggering to himself, he entered his office and closed the door behind him.

Robert made the coffee, answered phones, sorted the mail and never once regretted what he was doing. It felt appropriate, not a waste of his time. Gruffy was now awake and watched Robert with bemusement from his sentry box.

"I need a coffee, crab face," Gruffy said.

"Sorry, fresh out of Shakespearean coffee," Robert answered, with a smile.

"Shakespearean coffee?"

"Coffee brewed from the same beans that dreams are made of," Robert said as he playfully threw a rolled up ball of paper, hitting Gruffy in the head.

"Nice," said Gruffy, "real nice."

At lunchtime, Robert whisked downstairs to grab a takeout meal. Upon his return, Harding stood at his open office door.

You left your post?" he said to Robert.

"Gotta eat."

"Had to answer the phone myself," Harding said, expecting more of a mea culpa than he was getting from Robert. "There's a Miss Blessing on line two for you."

"I'll take it in my office," Robert said, knowing that it would concern Alison and secretly hoping that it wasn't going to be bad news. He was through his office door before he realized that he had walked straight through Gruffy's barrier. He stopped and turned to see Gruffy and the barrier begin to fade from view.

"This isn't over, cabbage breath," Gruffy said as he and the barrier vanished from sight.

Despite Gruff's protestations, Robert instinctively knew that Gruffy and the barrier were now gone for good. They had done their job, he reasoned, of being an external out-picturing of his internal state. The rage and anger that Gruffy and the barrier represented were not now present inside of him, in fact, deep within he felt a peaceful calm that he had not experienced since…well, he couldn't remember since when.

Dreams are such ingenious creations of the mind, he considered. They show up in your world as challenges when all they are are messages of the soul, showing you "out there" what is but a reflection of what is hidden "in here," deeply buried from view.

Picking up the phone, he pressed the flashing light on line two.

"Marjorie, it's Robert." Robert's sunny outlook slowly disappeared as he listened to the bad news from Miss Blessing. Alison was not well and had spent the day in bed, after being attended to by her physician. She was not expected to recover any time soon. Expressing his sympathies, Robert told her that he would visit after work.

Robert put all incoming phone calls to voice-mail while he saw just one client in the afternoon. Stopping off to get flowers first, Robert then drove to Alison's place. Sitting up in bed, Alison looked pale and exhausted. As Miss Blessing showed Robert into her bedroom, Alison perked up and smiled.

"How are you doing, princess?" Robert asked, handing her the flowers, which made her smile even more.

"They're beautiful," Alison said, appreciatively.

"No pressure but you need to get well," Robert said, smiling. "I'm starting a band and I could use a good cello player."

"You're starting a band? That's great," Alison said with enthusiasm.

"You'll need to brush up on those jazz standards," Robert said, "I'll make sure you get all the music."

"Great," Alison said, poorly hiding her uncertainty. "Hey," she said, and then added, "you worked reception for me today. That's the sweetest thing anyone, besides my mother, has ever done for me." Leaning forward, and gesturing for him to lean towards her, she kissed his cheek.

"Don't worry about a thing," Robert said, trying not to sound as sad as he felt. "I'll make sure that you don't get fired."

Aware that she was tiring, Robert told her to get some good rest and that he would visit again. As Miss Blessing showed him out, he turned to her, hoping to hear something hopeful about her condition.

"Alison's not looking too good to me. Does she get like this a lot?" he asked.

"I've never seen her this bad," Miss Blessing answered.

"What did the doctor say will pull her through his?"

"The same thing that pulls everybody through life, Robert. The will to live and the alignment of that will with the Will of God."

"Her doctor said that?" asked Robert, incredulously.

"No, her medical doctor gave her pills to take and said that they need to do more tests but that things didn't look good."

Oh, yeah, thought Robert, that sounds about right, that's pretty much doctor speak for 'we have no idea what's going on.' Robert had one more trip to make before he went home. He headed to the hospital to check in on his dad. As he drove in the direction of the hospital, he realized that he did not have the mental stamina to face his anxiety-ridden mother and comatose father, so soon after his visit with ailing Alison. Instead, he drove home and ordered in some Chinese food. After it was delivered and he had eaten, he ran a nice warm bath for himself. He lit some candles and put on some Bill Evans, suitably relaxing background music, then settled in for a nice long soak.

Robert's spontaneous 'me time' paid off handsomely. He felt stronger, at peace, and much more able to cope when he finally visited his father in the hospital.

"It's critical now, Robert," his mother greeted him when he entered the room. "He needs a kidney ASAP. You need to make the appointment."

"Okay," Robert said.

"You're going to do it, aren't you?"

"Of course," Robert answered just as his attention was diverted by the sight of the Elusive Lady who was passing by the window. "I'll be right back," he said as he gave pursuit.

"Where are you going?" Anita called after him.

Robert followed the Elusive Lady as she descended the stairs. Haven't we done this before, he thought to himself? Like before, Robert followed her into the morgue and again, once he got there, she was nowhere to be seen. He shivered slightly, a reaction to the cold temperature of the place. Robert called out to her, "Didn't we do this before? Hello? I got it the first time. The morgue represents death. I was dead inside. I got it, already."

This time, when he reached the body storage area, there was only a single body, on a gurney, covered by a sheet. Lifting the sheet to take a look, he got a shock he wasn't prepared for. It was Alison. Oh, no, this can't be right, he said to himself, this can't be right. Looking up and around, he yelled out loud, perhaps to the Elusive Lady, or perhaps to God:

"How can you explain this? This is one of the most alive people I've ever met…" Caught between a mix of outrage, anger and confusion, he found it hard to think straight. "My father is the most dead person I know. And he's still alive? Huh?" he asked, inarticulately. Touching Alison's face with tenderness he said, "Oh, Alison. You had so much to live for."

"So do you," a voice said. Quickly turning around, he saw the Elusive Lady standing peacefully and calmly. "Alison is in a beautiful place now."

"Are you real?" he asked her. Robert couldn't see her lips move; it was as if she was talking to him in his head.

"I'm as real as you are," she answered cryptically. "Are you real?"

"I don't know," he answered truthfully, "I'm confused." The Elusive Lady turned to go.

"Wait!" Robert called, causing her to stop and turn back around. With further confusion, he asked her, "You represent life and my father represents… death?"

He didn't see her smile but maybe she did.

"If your father were to represent anything, it would be forgiveness," she said, "he's only hanging on because he needs to have your forgiveness." Robert thought to himself, he wants my forgiveness? How can I forgive someone I despise?

"Why do you despise him?" she asked, as if being privy to his thoughts.

"He ruined my life," answered Robert, as if had reverted back to being a ten year old, "he was a rotten father."

"How good a father and husband have you been?" she asked pointedly and left.

Taken aback and increasingly aware of a terrible sense of guilt, tinged with shame, Robert dropped his head. He took a good look at Alison's pale small blue-white corpse and felt a little better knowing that she was now in a better place.

"Who am I to know what's fair and what's right, he asked himself? I've never hit Jason but have I really been the best of fathers? In twenty years time, will he be telling his therapist that I was a rotten father? Did Gail take Jason off on a cruise, and stay away so long, because I was a really great father and husband? Are the emotional hurts that I'm blaming my father for, the same hurts that, in turn, are hurting my wife and son? If I'm damaged, then, ipso facto, can I only raise a child the way a damaged person can raise a child? Unless I'm healed, the sins of the father will be visited upon the generations... my son?

When Robert went back upstairs and rejoined Anita, she was sitting, obviously exhausted, by his father's bed. He lovingly took her hands in his own.

"Why don't you go home, mom," he told her softly, "I'll sit with him."

"You're going to make the appointment?" she asked, desperately.

"First thing," he assured her.

"I knew that you'd do the right thing, son," she said. She looked as if a great weight had lifted from her shoulders, "We'll talk to the doctors tomorrow."

Robert kissed her forehead and bade her drive safely home. He sat down at his father's side and took his hand. His father looked peaceful to him now. Was that because he wasn't feeling so angry towards the man now? Calmly looking at his father in repose, he realized that they never had really talked very much at all, while he was growing up.

They had not seemed to be able to communicate in any meaningful, heart-to-heart way. Considering that, it dawned on him that he did not really know his father very well. In which case, he considered, it is a great shame, considering that here he is, on his death bed, and we may be unable to speak to each other, ever again. Feeling a wave of compassion and the love of a child for his father, Robert spoke quietly.

"I'm sorry that I let my anger and my judgment of you stand in the way of truly getting to know you; getting to know you as a person, as someone who has had challenges and disappointments…like any other person on this planet," Robert said quietly to his father. "I don't even know what kind of childhood you had, what you were like, as a kid. I know your father was tough—I think you may have said that he drank? Or did he hit you when he was drunk?" Robert shook his head, almost ashamed of knowing so little about this person who meant so much to him.

"What kind of an idiot have I been," he admonished himself, "self-righteous and justified for holding a grudge against you, for allowing my anger to get in the way of any meaningful connection between us. I remember laughing when Heathcliff, I think it was, asked me once if I went out often and had a beer with you, if that was one of the things we did together.

"I couldn't think of anything I'd like to do more, right now. I would so love to take you down to Wallace's Bar, or any bar for that matter, order a couple of beers and talk. You could tell me about you growing up, what you wanted to be when you were little, heck, just talk about anything…the weather, the Cubs, anything…" Robert trailed off and really feeling his heart soften and open, he allowed his tears to flow freely. Unbeknownst to him, the Elusive Lady stood behind him, a loving presence with a supportive hand pressed onto his shoulder.

"I just kept thinking, if only you had told me that you loved me, if only you'd tell me that you were proud of me, that I was enough for you, to be proud of… and because you didn't, I hated you for it… and I felt justified that I hated you because you just wouldn't say those things to me…" Robert choked up and looked in vain for a tissue for his nose and eyes.

"But how could you? You couldn't, could you? Because you were damaged, weren't you? You were probably so fucked up, you wouldn't have known love or kindness if it jumped up and bit you on the nose. You probably got the crap beat out of you every day of your childhood life, by a father that genuinely did hate your guts. I'm sure you weren't good enough for him. I bet that he probably never once said that he was proud of you… I don't know. And that's just it, I don't know. I don't know about anything anymore… so how can I judge you? The joke here is that I can't remember the last time I told Jason that I was proud of him. How's that for irony?" Robert pressed his father's hand tighter.

"I guess what I'm trying to say is that I'm sorry. I'm sorry and I forgive you. You were probably doing the very best that you knew how to do and I can't blame you for any of my screw ups. I don't blame you for anything, anymore."

Robert got a fright when he felt movement in his father's hand. Groggily, his father's eyes opened very slightly. Robert panicked. Was he imagining this, he's been unresponsive for weeks? But it felt as if his father wanted him to lean forward, closer to him, so Robert did.

"I love you, son," his father whispered, or at least that's what Robert thought he heard him say.

"I love you, too, dad," Robert said and then his father went back to sleep.

The dream is a lie, but the dreaming is true.

~Robert Penn Warren

When Robert entered his house, he smiled broadly when he saw Gail's suitcase and travel bag in the hall. When Jason came running down to him, Robert scooped him up into his arms and hugged him tightly.

"Am I glad to see you!" Robert said, swinging him around. Lowering him down to his level, Robert looked his son in the eyes and spoke slowly and clearly.

"I love you, Jason. I love you and I'm proud of you."

"Me too, dad. I'm proud of you, too," Jason answered awkwardly.

Looking radiant, relaxed and confident, glowing from what had obviously been a deeply rejuvenating vacation, Gail stood watching from the doorway. Walking towards her, Robert noticed a striking similarity between Gail and the Elusive Lady.

"I had forgotten how absolutely beautiful you are," he said to his wife.

"I'm sorry for leaving like that," Gail said as a prelude to the speech which she had mentally prepared and felt obligated to start with. Robert, however, placed a finger to her lips.

"I'm the one that's sorry," he said, softly. "I turned into a big jerk, didn't I?"

"I didn't leave because you were a big jerk," she said, smiling. "I was confused, tired, feeling really down, and not well. It turns out... I saw the ship's doctor... I'm pregnant."

Robert hugged his wife and lifted her up with complete joy and surprise.

"Oh, sweetie, I love you so much, that's great news! Come here, son," Robert said hustling Jason into the group hug, "you're going to have a sister!"

"Mom said I was going to have a brother?" Jason replied, confused.

"A boy!" Robert exclaimed. "It's a boy?! Then you'll have a brother!" His enthusiasm was infectious as Robert twirled them around in a happy dance. Suddenly, he stopped moving and collapsed to the floor. It was if a switch had been thrown and had the effect of powering him down. Everything began to fade. Blackness crept in.

"Honey, what's wrong?" Gail bent down with concern.

Robert was losing consciousness; in his inner vision everything spun around, as if he were caught up in some tornado of the mind. It was taking him away and he was powerless to break free. Like a blind man in free fall, he flailed his mental arms in the hopes of grabbing something to hold onto. The force was too great and he was too small. He was swept away to some place dark and empty. Maybe this is what being in a void feels like, was his last thought. Then his world went black and silent.

******

The darkness broke. A faint light intruded upon Robert's consciousness. Everything was out of focus but groggily Robert vaguely make out what appeared to be his father's hospital room; except that, curiously, now he was the one lying in the bed.

"Are you awake, Dr. Monro?" he heard a voice say as a white figure approached.

******

The nurse helped Robert to sit up in bed as Gail and Jason entered, looking joyful. The left side of his face felt both numb and swollen and his left arm and his left leg were in casts.

"You're awake!" Gail declared with happiness.

"Daddy, daddy!" Jason said, not knowing how else to express his delight.

"I was in an accident?" Robert asked, his mind still in a haze.

"We almost lost you," Gail said, "don't you remember? At that intersection you hate?"

A flash of memory suddenly ripped through his mind. He could see himself at the four-way stop intersection; he was shouting at the bad driver lady. Losing his patience, he had finally pulled right out into the intersection and then bam! He got sideswiped hard by a colossal SUV which had run right through the intersection. As the SUV pushed his car across the street, and into something else, glass breaking, metal screeching, the airbags deployed and everything had gone dark.

"We're taking the drunk driver to court," Gail said, as Robert checked out his injuries.

"How long was I...?"

"Six weeks," answered Gail quickly.

"Six weeks?" repeated Robert in amazement.

"We've been with you, every day, haven't we, Jason?" said Gail supportively.

"We've been reading you stories," added Jason as he showed Robert his book collection, *Alice In Wonderland* and *The Wizard Of Oz* being two titles among them.

"We read that talking to people who are in comas is really helpful, darling," Gail said as she squeezed Robert's good hand tighter and looked lovingly into her husband's eyes.

"And playing music," said Jason holding up some CDs of Jazz and cello music.

"You guys thought of everything," Robert said, with appreciation.

Robert was startled by the sight of both his parents coming through the door, secretly delighted to see his father looking fairly healthy for his age. Curiously, his father walked more slowly than normal and seemed to be favoring one side of his body.

"We knew you'd come back to us," Anita said, tearfully, "we were so worried."

"You can't keep a good man down. Isn't that right, son?" Franklin beamed.

"You're looking great, dad," said Robert.

"He's looking great, now, thank God," added Anita, holding her man tighter.

"What do you mean, 'now?'" asked Robert and then addressed his dad, "have you not been well?"

A wave of what looked like embarrassment circulated among Gail, Franklin and Anita, as if they were harboring a secret that they were not sure should be divulged.

"What?" asked Robert, sensing subterfuge, "did something happen?"

The three co-conspirators looked shyly to each other, perhaps wondering who should be the one to talk. Robert got more distressed.

"What is it? Someone please tell me," he almost pleaded.

"Your left kidney got damaged, son," Anita finally proffered, "it had to be replaced or…" It was obviously too distressing for her to finish the sentence without her bursting into tears, which on this happy occasion, she was loathe to do.

"We weren't going to tell you, right away," said Gail, helping out.

"I had a kidney transplant?" said Robert, figuring it out. No one disagreed. Robert mentally felt around where the new kidney would be to see if he could tell what difference, if any, could be discerned. Right then, he didn't feel any apparent disparity. Suddenly, as if he were struck by a bolt of lightning, he stared directly at his smiling father and blurted out, "you gave me one of your kidneys!"

The other three adults smiled as if the revelation of their shared secret conferred upon them a sense of relief and renewed sense of group togetherness.

"His was a perfect match and he didn't think twice," Anita said with great pride as she squeezed her husband's arm even tighter.

"There was no way we could have waited… " started Gail and then stopped with concern for her husband when she saw him lurch forward as if he were in terrible agony. "Robert, are you alright?" she asked as she leaned closer to him, looking up at the machines to see if anything untoward like a flashing light, or a spike in the graph on a monitor, could give some indication as to why her husband was now retching with pain.

"I think it's a lot for him to take in, Gail," Anita said helpfully, "this is all too much for him, so soon."

Overcome with emotion, tears flowed down Robert's cheeks. "I love you all so very much," was all that he could manage to say.

Those who dream by day are cognizant of many things which escape those who dream only by night.

~Edgar Allan Poe

Eighteen months passed by and if he were asked, Robert would probably have said that they were the most rewarding and love-filled moments of his life. His physical wounds had healed; his practice was thriving; he was never so much in love with his wife and his son and his infant son, Franklin Jr.

After introducing his father to the nuances of jazz trios, Franklin became something of an aficionado. Every Sunday afternoon, come rain or shine, he accompanied Robert to Wallace's bar to hang out, chew the fat and listen to that week's performers in the Sunday Afternoon Trio series.

He also came on Monday nights, to hear his son play with the Munchkin City Jazz Group. It was a trio started by Robert. He played trumpet and clarinet. Alison Blessing was featured on double bass. Dr. Richard Harding played drums. They hadn't set the world on fire yet, hence their Monday night slot, but then that was never their intention. They loved to play and cover the old standards in their own inimitable way.

Robert doesn't keep a dream journal and a day journal anymore. Ever since his coma, he has kept only one journal, a life journal. He no longer distinguishes between what he sees in his dream life to what he sees in his waking life as separate or different but instead accords everything that he sees, feels, hears or intuits as having equal significance and subject to observation and if necessary, deeper scrutiny and analysis.

In the process of coauthoring a book with Miss Marjorie Blessing, they never even refer to dreams as dreams but rather like to refer to them as experiences of the heart and mind. As their understanding grows, they are developing a new theory that posits that a life lived with an open heart and mind can access all aspects of self, of experienced reality and of the imagination and that the language that each actuality speaks – symbol and metaphor – can be understood and hence the heretofore mysteries of the mind and of consciousness itself can be demystified and decoded. When asked about their theories and their evolving understanding, they have been known to answer that patience is a virtue and just like their book, we are all works in progress.

ABOUT THE AUTHOR

Dermot Davis is an award-winning playwright, having had plays performed in Dublin, Boston and Los Angeles. His creative work encompasses varied genres and styles — drama, comedy, and, more recently, sci-fi, with a special focus on human themes and characters transformed by life experience. A sometimes actor, he is a co-founder of the Laughing Gravy Theatre (which performed Irish Vaudeville and excerpts of Irish literary works as well as drama, including the original stage plays of Mr. Davis) where he and other members of the troupe were artists-in-residence at the Piccolo Spoleto Festival in Charleston, South Carolina. He currently resides in Los Angeles. Follow him on his Goodreads.com Author Page at http://www.goodreads.com/author/show/6565450.Dermot_Davis.

OTHER BOOKS BY DERMOT DAVIS:

Zen and Sex (a Romantic Comedy)
Brain: The Man That Wrote the Book That
Changed the World

Made in the USA
Middletown, DE
09 December 2014